# Charm Club

*Please return Isabella Streetbecker*

# love

# stone

## Belinda Ray

SCHOLASTIC INC.

New York  Toronto  London  Auckland  Sydney
Mexico City  New Delhi  Hong Kong  Buenos Aires

*For my nieces, Krista, Danica, and Jaime, who are all strong, intelligent, and beautiful young women.*
*—BR*

ISBN 0-439-77516-7

ALLOYENTERTAINMENT   Produced by Alloy Entertainment
151 West 26th Street, New York, NY 10001

SCHOLASTIC and associated logos are trademarks and/or registered trademarks of Scholastic Inc.

12  11  10 9 8 7 6                    7 8 9 10 11/0

Printed in the U.S.A.                    40
First printing, January 2006

# CHAPTER
## One

"There are already six eighth graders on the squad," explained Becky Pelchek, who happened to be one of them, "and we usually have about sixteen cheerleaders, so that means there are ten spots open."

Jenna Scott flipped her long, blonde hair over her shoulder and glanced casually at the rest of the girls seated on the bleachers. By her count there were twelve eighth graders, fourteen seventh graders, and three sixth graders, including her. Twenty-nine girls competing for ten spots on the cheerleading squad.

*That's not bad,* Jenna thought. *A third of us will make it.* Of course, that also meant two-thirds of them wouldn't, but Jenna didn't think she'd wind up in that part of the equation. While it was true that sixth graders didn't typically make the team, Jenna knew that she wasn't a typical sixth grader. She was already in with most of the older girls, plus she'd taken years of dance and gymnastics lessons so she knew it would be easy for her to pick up all the moves. The other two sixth graders who were trying out, on the other hand, were probably out of luck.

Michelle Burton and Lucy Greene were definitely peppy enough to be cheerleaders. They both had curly ringlets of hair—Michelle's bright red and Lucy's blonde—and they both smiled constantly, but neither one of them had friends outside of the sixth grade, which was a definite strike against them. Sixth graders were at the bottom of the social ladder at Adams Middle School and, without an ally in the seventh or eighth grades, it was hard to climb any higher.

Jenna turned her attention back to Becky, who was explaining how tryouts would work.

"Over the next week, you'll all be taught two cheers, and then, a week from today—" Becky stopped and turned around, interrupted by the sound of heels clicking across the gym floor. "Are you here for the cheerleading meeting?" she asked.

Jenna saw her two best friends, Emily Reisman and Sarah Robbins, scurrying toward the bleachers, and she dropped her head into her hands. *What are* they *doing here?* she wondered. They knew she had a study group meeting and they were supposed to meet her *afterward*, not—

"Yes. We're here for the meeting," Emily said.

*What?* Jenna thought. They hadn't said anything to her about trying out for the cheerleading team.

"Sorry we're late," Sarah added.

Becky Pelchek didn't look amused. She scowled at the two girls then turned to her audience and said, "Just so you all know, sixth graders have even less of a chance of making the team when they show up late." Most of the girls on the bleachers laughed. Even Emily and Sarah managed nervous giggles as they made their way toward the bleachers, but Jenna wasn't smiling. They were planning to sit with her. She could tell from the way they kept trying to make eye contact, but she didn't want to be associated with them. Not only had they come in late, they were *sixth graders*. Jenna had snagged herself a seat between Andrea Killiard and Molly O'Connell, two popular eighth graders, and she didn't need Emily and Sarah reminding them that she was two years younger than they were.

So instead of making room for Emily and Sarah, Jenna pulled her green-and-blue messenger bag up onto the bleachers in front of her and pretended to go through it, taking up as much space as she possibly could. It didn't take Emily and Sarah long to realize that there wasn't enough room for them to sit near Jenna, so they switched direction and took up some empty bench space on the other end.

*Phew,* thought Jenna, placing her bag back at her feet. *That was close.* She shifted her weight left and right, trying to get comfortable, but there was something sticking into her leg. She reached into the front pocket of her jeans and pulled out the charm bracelet she'd found on the gym floor on her way into the meeting. She examined each of its charms—a unicorn, a princess, a fairy, two gemstones, and an angel. *That must be what it was,* Jenna thought, feeling the tip of the angel's wings with her index finger. They were pretty sharp.

Jenna tilted the bracelet in her hand, watching it sparkle as it reflected the fluorescent lights of the gym. It was too bad she couldn't keep it for herself, but she knew that whoever had lost it would want it back, and turning it into the lost and found was the right thing to do. *Still,* Jenna thought, admiring the bracelet, *it would be nice to have one of my own.* Maybe she could get her mother to buy her one for her birthday or something.

Jenna took one last look at the silver bracelet and then dropped it into her bag. She'd take it to the lost and found right after the cheering meeting.

"As I was saying," Becky Pelchek went on once Emily and Sarah were settled, "you'll all be taught two cheers over the next week. We'll practice them as a group, and then each of you will have a chance to perform the cheers in front of a panel of judges who will decide who makes the squad."

"How many judges are there?" a seventh grader asked.

"And who are they?" added one of the eighth graders who wasn't already on the team.

"There are five," Becky answered. "Ms. Fine, our coach; two teachers—I think it's going to be Ms. Garcia and Ms. Rainey this year; and two eighth graders—me and Lindsay Wissink." Becky and Lindsay were the obvious choices for captains of the cheerleading squad. Both of them had been on the team since they were in sixth grade.

"And now, if there aren't any more questions . . ." Becky paused for a moment, scanning the bleachers, but no hands were raised. "Lindsay and I will demonstrate the cheers for you."

Lindsay walked out to join Becky in front of the bleachers, and the two of them stood mannequin-still for about three seconds. Then, with no signal that Jenna could detect, they both began moving in unison, shouting out words and executing arm and leg movements in sync.

When they finished both cheers, everyone in the bleachers applauded enthusiastically, including Jenna, even though she wasn't all that impressed. Becky and Lindsay were good cheerleaders and all, but Jenna had seen plenty of spots where each of them could stand to improve.

For one thing, Becky needed to keep her arms a little stiffer. The way she let them swing around made her look sloppy. And Lindsay's right leg bent every time she kicked. They were small details, Jenna knew, but if they were going to be teaching the cheers, they should have had them down perfectly.

"Okay, so that's it for today," Becky said when the applause had died down. "But we'll meet right after school every day for the next week to learn the cheers. If you have any other questions, Lindsay and I will be hanging out for a while. Otherwise, you can go."

Jenna glanced at Molly and Andrea. "I don't have any questions. Do you?" she asked with a smile.

"No, but I'm a little nervous about cheering in front of a *panel*," Molly said. "That's going to be weird."

"It won't be that bad," Jenna said. "Besides,

if you make the squad, you'll be cheering in front of a whole gym full of people."

"Yeah," Molly agreed, "but they won't be deciding whether or not I can be on the team." "That's true," Andrea said. "Knowing that people are judging you makes it harder."

"I guess," Jenna said, although she wasn't particularly nervous about the tryouts. She'd always enjoyed performing in front of other people, and even though she'd only seen the cheers once, she was pretty sure she could already do them. With a week of practice, she'd have them down cold.

Over Molly's shoulder, Jenna saw Emily and Sarah approaching. "Um, I have to get going," she told Molly and Andrea. "My mom's picking me up and I have to stop by my locker before she gets here. But I'll see you guys at practice tomorrow, okay?"

"Sure."

"Yeah, see you tomorrow, Jenna."

Quickly, Jenna turned and began walking out of the gym. It wasn't until she was at the door that Emily and Sarah caught up to her.

"Jenna, wait!" Emily called, her heels once again clicking on the floor. Reluctantly, Jenna stopped—but not until she was in the hallway. She didn't want any of the older girls to see her talking to the two sixth graders who had shown up late.

"So? What do you think?" Sarah asked.

"We're trying out for the cheerleading squad!" Emily squealed.

"Wouldn't it be cool if all three of us made it?"

Jenna looked at her friends. Their eyes were wide and their grins were broad. They were really excited about this. "Yeah, that would be cool," Jenna said halfheartedly. *It would also be a miracle,* she thought to herself. Emily and Sarah weren't exactly the most coordinated girls around, and they weren't incredibly popular either. The only reason anyone knew who they were was because they had started hanging out with Jenna this year. If they were in seventh grade, being Jenna's friends might be enough to get them on the cheerleading squad, but in sixth grade they needed natural talent, too. And Jenna didn't think that either one of them had it.

"When did you decide to try out?" Jenna asked. "You didn't say anything in math class when I told you I was going to the meeting."

Emily and Sarah exchanged grins. "Well," Emily started, "we were kind of talking about it on the phone last night, but neither one of us was sure we'd have the guts."

"Then, in math, when you said you were trying out, we both sort of thought, why not?"

"So we talked about it after school and finally decided to do it."

"A little late," Sarah added, "but at least we got there, and that's what's important, right?"

"Yeah," Jenna said. "Sure." *But being on time would have been better.*

"So, what are you doing now?" Emily asked. "My mom is picking up me and Sarah and dropping us at the mall for an hour or so. Do you want to come?"

Jenna glanced toward the gym and saw that Molly, Andrea, and a few other eighth graders were headed for the door. "Um, no thanks," she said. "My mom's already on her way and she'll be mad if I don't need a ride."

"Your mom? Mad?" Sarah asked, stunned. Jenna's mom never got mad about anything. She was one of the most easygoing parents around.

"Yeah, she's kind of been in a bad mood this week," Jenna lied. She looked back at the gym. Molly and the others were getting closer. "I'll see you guys tomorrow, okay?" she said, backing away. And without waiting for their response, she turned and speed-walked away.

Jenna could feel Sarah and Emily watching her as she continued down the hall, but she didn't turn around. She'd been a little abrupt with them, she knew, but they'd get over it. They always did.

As Jenna approached the office, she slipped

her hand into her front pocket and pulled out the bracelet. "Too bad I can't keep you," she mumbled, holding the chain between her thumb and forefinger. She was just about to step into the office when she was stopped by two voices.

"It's a silver bracelet with a bunch of charms on it," the first voice said.

"An angel, a unicorn, a fairy, a princess, and two gems," the second voice added.

"Are you sure nobody's turned it in?" the first voice asked.

Jenna flattened herself against the wall just outside the office and listened. *Amanda Littlefield and Keisha Johnson*, she thought, gazing down at the bracelet. It belonged to one of them.

"I don't have any bracelets in the lost and found right now," responded Mr. Knight, one of the school secretaries. "But I can write down your description, and if anything comes in I'll have you paged to the office. Which one of you does the bracelet belong to, anyway?"

"Me," Amanda and Keisha said at the same time.

In the hall, Jenna squinted. Didn't they even know which one of them owned the bracelet?

Mr. Knight was obviously puzzled, too. "It belongs to both of you?" he asked.

"Sort of," Keisha said.

"We kind of share it," Amanda added. "It's a good-luck bracelet."

Silently, Jenna shook her head. The bracelet was good luck and they shared it. Of course. They were so . . . *weird*, so immature. Still, the bracelet was theirs and Jenna knew she should return it to them. But something was keeping her from walking into the office and giving it back.

Jenna gazed down at the bracelet, knowing that if it belonged to anyone else, she would go into the office and return it without hesitation. But it didn't belong to anyone else. It belonged to Keisha and Amanda, and they'd been getting on Jenna's nerves a lot lately.

Normally, Jenna didn't even notice people like Amanda and Keisha. They weren't popular, they weren't trendy, and they didn't have any cool friends or ties to older kids. For the most part, they hung around with each other and a geeky seventh-grade boy named Sam Sullivan. They weren't in Jenna's social circle and they probably never would be. They were the kind of people Jenna couldn't possibly have cared less about. Until they started causing her so much grief.

First, Jenna's crush, Noah Carpenter, had started showing interest in Keisha, of all people. She was pretty—in her own way—but she was boring. Simple sweaters and jeans, hair pulled back into a ponytail, no unique accessories or makeup. Jenna couldn't figure out what Noah saw in her.

And Amanda—sheesh! Amanda had beaten Jenna in a student council race, which was completely humiliating. Jenna was the most popular girl in the sixth grade, and yet she'd lost to Amanda, who dressed like a poster girl for a remedial fashion school. True, her outfits weren't boring, like Keisha's, but they weren't exactly cool, either—at least not by Jenna's standards. Knee-highs and clogs? Black T-shirts with plaid skirts and combat boots? *Please.* How she ever got elected to student council was a total mystery to Jenna.

"If anyone turns it in I'll let you know," Mr. Knight said.

Jenna clutched the bracelet in her hand and thought quickly. Returning the bracelet was the right thing to do. She knew it. So that's what she would do. *Eventually.* Being without the bracelet for a day or two wouldn't hurt Amanda and Keisha. It would just make them squirm a little and keep them preoccupied.

*And,* Jenna thought as she tiptoed down the hall, *maybe that will keep them out of my way for a while.*

# CHAPTER
## Two

"Hey! / Get with it! / Let's take it to the limit! / Fire it up and feel the heat! / Clap your hands to the beat! / Go Adams, go Adams! / Go, go, go Adams!"

Jenna finished the cheer with a jump called a front hurdler—both arms forward, one leg straight out in front, and the other bent underneath her body. *Not bad,* she thought, checking her reflection in the full-length mirror that hung on the back of her bedroom door. It was only her third time through the cheer and she already had it down pretty good. By next week it would be perfect. But the second cheer was a little more complicated.

With her legs together and her arms at her side, Jenna got ready to start the second cheer. "Ready? O-kay!" she said, imitating the call-and-response cheerleaders often used to make sure everyone started at the same time. Then, stretching her arms out wide and bending her knees, she began the cheer.

"We heard it through the grapevine / that your team is pretty tough! / But when you're up against the Falcons / tough is not enough! / We've got pride and spirit / Adams is the name! / We're on the move, and out to prove / we're gonna win this game!"

The second cheer ended with a high straddle jump called a toe touch, which Jenna executed perfectly, but that was no surprise. She'd had excellent straddle, tuck, and pike jumps since third grade when she'd first started taking gymnastics.

Her instructor, Kana Terauchi, who also coached the local team, was always trying to get Jenna to compete. According to Kana, Jenna had the perfect gymnast's body—compact and strong. But joining the team would have meant hours of practice every day, and Jenna hadn't wanted to limit herself to gymnastics alone. So, over the years she took lessons off and on, alternating gymnastics with various dance classes—ballet, jazz, street funk, or whatever else interested her at the moment. And now, all of those classes were going to pay off. She was going to be one of those rare

Adams students who made the cheerleading squad on the first try.

Jenna grinned at herself in the mirror and then let her eyes stray to the reflection of her messenger bag, which was leaning against her bed. She walked over to it and reached inside to find the charm bracelet she'd brought home from school—the one that belonged to Amanda and Keisha.

Running it through her fingers, Jenna examined each of the charms again, wondering if Amanda and Keisha had added all of them to the bracelet, and if so, in what order. It seemed that the angel must have come first because she was right in the middle. But Jenna wasn't sure which charm may have come next. *Maybe the fairy,* she thought. *Or the unicorn.* They were each midway between the angel and one end of the bracelet, which seemed like a good place for a second or third charm.

Jenna circled the bracelet around her wrist and clasped it there, admiring it. "If I had one of these, I'd wear it everyday," she said to herself, and as soon as the words were out of her mouth she began to feel guilty. Realizing how much she enjoyed wearing the bracelet had made her wonder how she would feel if it actually were *hers* and she had lost it.

*Maybe I should give it back to Amanda and Keisha,* she thought, moving the bracelet around her wrist. They were probably worried that they'd lost it for good. *But they haven't,* Jenna reminded herself. It wasn't like she was planning on keeping it forever.

Jenna unclasped the bracelet and held it in her hand, feeling its weight. Then she glanced at the alarm clock on her nightstand. Five-thirty. In another half hour her mother would be calling her down for dinner, and after that she'd have to start her homework. She didn't have time to think about the bracelet right now. She needed to practice her cheers.

Jenna walked over to her bureau, and opened the wooden music box where she kept her jewelry. As usual, the tiny cupid popped up as she opened the top and began to spin to the tune of "Can't Help Falling in Love," by Elvis Presley. Smiling, Jenna watched the golden figure make a few revolutions before tossing the bracelet in and closing the top.

The outside of the music box was painted with faded pink roses and golden braids that had worn off in places over time. She'd had it since she was six years old, when her favorite aunt, Cynthia, had given it to her as a birthday present. Jenna knew it was kind of cutesy, and sometimes she even hid it away when she had friends over, but she still loved the music box—especially its spinning cherub.

Most of the music boxes she'd seen had ballerinas that spun around with the music. She'd never seen another one with a cupid, and she knew that Aunt Cynthia had chosen it for her for exactly that reason—because it was special, just as Aunt Cynthia always said Jenna was.

Jenna patted the box with her hand once and then returned to the mirror. She centered herself, placed her arms flat against the sides of her body, and bent her knees. "Ready?" she called, "O-kay! We heard it through the grapevine / that your team is pretty tough. / But when you're up against the Falcons / tough is not enough!" Jenna was just about to launch into the second half of the cheer—arms overhead, legs locked—when she was interrupted by a loud knock.

Sighing, she let her arms drop to her sides and called, "Come in!" Jenna watched the door to her room, waiting for her mother to enter. Her father wasn't home and her older brother never knocked.

Jenna waited, but after ten seconds, the door was still closed. "Come in!" she called again, more forcefully this time. But still, no one opened the door. With a frustrated huff, Jenna walked over to the door and flung it open. "I said *come in*," she snapped, but there was no one there. Jenna scrunched her eyebrows together and leaned out into the hallway. She glanced left, toward the staircase, and right, toward her parents' room, her brother's room, and the bathroom, but she didn't see anyone.

"Huh," Jenna muttered, stepping back into her room and closing the door again. Maybe she was just hearing things.

She went back to the mirror and centered herself again, striking the pose she'd been in before she'd been interrupted. Then, bending her left arm so that her fist was in front of her heart and straightening her right arm out to the side, she continued the cheer. "We've got pride and spirit! / Adams is the name! / We're on the move, and out to prove—"

Again, before she could finish the cheer, Jenna was interrupted by another knock. "What is it?" she demanded, marching straight to her door and flinging it open. Once again, there was no one there. "What the—?" Jenna muttered. And then she heard it again. But this time she realized that the knocking noise was coming from inside her bedroom.

She took a few steps toward her bed and

waited, listening carefully. Sure enough, there was another knock, louder this time, and coming from somewhere near her bureau. Slowly, Jenna crept toward the side of her room, wondering what on earth could be making that noise. *A mouse, maybe?* she thought, shuddering. Maybe she should go get her mother. But they'd never had trouble with mice before. Jenna's mother had three cats, Precious, Kitty, and Doofus—Jenna had named the last one— and they'd kept the household mouse-free for years. But if it wasn't a mouse, what could it be?

For a moment, Jenna stood staring at her bureau, completely stumped. Then her eyes fell on her music box, and she remembered that once before when she'd closed its top, the cupid had somehow managed to keep spinning, occasionally knocking itself against the lid.

"Duh," she muttered to herself as she walked over and flipped it open. As always, "Can't Help Falling in Love" started playing and the cupid began to spin, but Jenna could see that he was a little crooked—probably because the bracelet had caught one of his arms when Jenna had tossed it into the box.

"Sorry about that," Jenna said, reaching for the bracelet. But before she could grab it, the little cupid came free of his stand and stumbled across the box's pink satin lining, tripped over the rim, and then fell and landed in a heap on Jenna's bureau, his bow and arrow lying at his feet.

Jenna watched, stunned, as the tiny figure, which had somehow changed from a solid gold statue into a tiny pink-fleshed boy with large blue eyes, curly blonde hair, and soft feathery wings in a flowing white toga, rubbed his head.

"Whew!" he exclaimed, blinking up at Jenna. "You have no idea how dizzy six years of spinning will make you!"

# CHAPTER
## Three

"What . . . *who* . . . what—?" Jenna stammered.

The tiny cupid stood up and walked to the edge of the bureau. "Marcus Trebellius Maximus is the name," he declared with a modest bow. "*Aaaaand*"—he continued, scurrying to retrieve his bow and arrow—"love is my game!" With a wide grin and a dramatic flourish of his arms, he inserted the arrow into the bow and drew it back.

He held this pose for a moment, glancing sideways at Jenna with twinkling blue eyes. It seemed as though he was waiting for applause or some kind of recognition, but Jenna could only stare at the tiny winged boy, unable to believe her eyes. "Marcus . . . Tre-*what*-ius?" she asked.

The cupid sighed and let his bow drop, replacing the arrow in the pouch on his back.

"Tre-BELL-ee-us MAX-i-mus," he said, slowly pronouncing each syllable. "I work with the Noble Order of Cupid, helping to spread love and joy around the world. Or at least I used to—before . . . *the accident*," he added, whispering.

For a moment, the little cupid appeared despondent, but only for a moment. Then the twinkle returned to his eyes. "But I'm free now!" he exclaimed with a boyish giggle. He began prancing around the top of Jenna's dresser executing small leaps and turns, fluttering his downy wings, and singing out the word *free* every time his feet left the ground.

Jenna watched in amazement. The tiny winged boy was a little larger than her index finger, but not by much. Still, he was quick on his feet and his jumps were quite graceful, which was surprising considering his footwear. And his build.

He was wearing large, flat sandals that stayed on his feet thanks to a series of crisscrossing leather straps that came halfway up his calves. Jenna couldn't imagine dancing in those shoes, let alone leaping around the way this little sprite was. And he was nearly as wide as he was tall!

His chubby little legs, arms, and cheeks were all rosy pink and fleshy, like the skin of a newborn baby, and he was so round it seemed to Jenna that he probably could have tucked himself into a ball and rolled a great distance. But despite his plumpness, this little cupid could move! His tiny white wings never stopped fluttering, and his little legs were running even when he was in the air.

Jenna watched him flitting about and rubbed her temples. "I've got to be dreaming," she told herself. It was ridiculous to think otherwise. Little music box people did *not* spin off their pedestals and start leaping around jubilantly.

Jenna squinted and glanced toward the mirror, trying to get a handle on the situation. "Okay, so I was cheering," she muttered, staring at the patch of rose-colored carpet where she'd been standing. "And there was a knocking noise." She turned her gaze to the music box, where the pedestal and the small spring that held it up were still spinning to the tune of the ice-cream truck–like music. Quickly, she snapped the lid closed and placed her palms together in front of her face. "I must have hit my head," she mumbled. It was the only thing that made sense.

"That's it. I was cheering, and I fell, and now I'm unconscious," she told herself, but even as she said it she knew she was wide awake. "Or maybe I have a concussion and I'm hallucinating or something?" she tried, but she didn't feel dizzy or even have a mild headache. Gingerly, Jenna felt her scalp, expecting—and half hoping—to find a huge bump, but there was nothing. And yet, when she looked at her bureau, the little cupid was still standing there, vibrant and vital, and still bounding around.

"Borrrrrrrrrn free!" he crooned. "As free as the wind blows! As free as the grass grows!"

Jenna dropped her hands to her sides, balling them into little fists, and eyed the giddy cupid. "What are you?" she demanded, fixing him with a stony stare.

The small boy stopped mid-leap, fluttering his wings and lowering himself gently onto the bureau. "I'm not a *what*," he said with a jolly grin. "I'm a *who*. Marcus Trebellius Maximus," he stated again, saying the name with pride. "But you can call me Max—most people do."

*This can't be happening,* Jenna thought. *It has to be a trick or—.* Jenna narrowed her eyes. *A trick.* That's exactly what it had to be. "All right, *Max*," she said, with an edge to her voice. Why hadn't she thought of it before? It was so obvious. Her older brother, Jason, loved to play tricks on her, and this had to be one of his best ever. How he was doing it, Jenna wasn't sure, but she was going to find out. "I'll ask you again. What are you? A puppet? A robot? Some kind of computer-generated thingy?"

Max took a step back on the bureau, his grin losing some luster. "I told you. I'm one of Cupid's assistants. I belong to the Noble Order of Cupid and I help to spread—"

"Yeah, yeah. Joy and love," Jenna scoffed. "Is that the story you're sticking with?"

"It's not a story, it's—"

"I don't know how you're doing this, Jason!" Jenna yelled, turning her head toward her bedroom door, "but if you don't get in here and explain it to me before I count to three, I'm going to break your little dolly in two!"

Jenna waited for a response from the other side of the hallway. She was positive her brother was hiding out in his bedroom and controlling the little "cupid" from there. No other explanation made sense, and it would be just like him to try to freak her out with a hoax like this. It was a good one, she had to admit, but she wasn't going to let him make her look like a fool.

"Did you hear me Jason?" she yelled, waiting for an answer. When there was no response Jenna turned back to the little cupid and began counting. "One . . . two . . . THREE!"

"I spread love and joy!" the cupid cried.

"Save it for Mom, Jason," Jenna sneered, reaching out to grab the tiny figure. Quickly, she snatched him off the bureau, and then, even more quickly, she dropped him and staggered backward with a gasp.

"Oh, my—you're ... you're ... you're *REAL!*" The feel of his warm body wriggling in her hand like a hamster had finally convinced her that he was neither a figment of her imagination nor a creation of her brother's twisted mind.

"Of course I am!" the cupid shouted back from behind the music box. At the sound of Jenna's yelp he had retreated almost as quickly as she had.

Jenna stared at him, her mouth hanging open. "But—that's impossible," she said after a moment. "You're a statue. You've been in my music box for six years. You can't be ... *alive.*"

"And yet," the boyish figure said, emerging from his hiding place, "I am." He placed both hands on his bow in front of him and, using it like a cane, did a little jig. At the end, he clicked his heels on both sides to drive the point home.

Jenna shook her head. She was still having trouble grasping the concept even though she knew it had to be true.

"Jenna! Are you all right?" Mrs. Scott asked as she rushed into the room.

"Huh? Oh, yeah, I'm fine, Mom," Jenna said, her eyes darting from the dancing cupid on her bureau to her mother and back again.

"What is it?" Mrs. Scott asked, following the direction of Jenna's gaze. "What's wrong?"

Obviously her mother couldn't see the little winged figure standing there with a bow and arrow. If she could, she probably would have screamed even louder than Jenna had.

"I, um . . ." Jenna contemplated telling the truth, but she knew her mother would never believe her. One word about the tiny cupid staring back at her, and Jenna's mother would have her wrapped in blankets with a thermometer jammed down her throat and an ambulance on the way. "I thought I saw a spider," Jenna said, "but it was just a piece of lint."

"Oh," Mrs. Scott said with a sigh. "Well, thank goodness. That was quite a scream. You scared me."

"Sorry," Jenna said.

Her mother turned to leave the room then stopped. "Oh, Jenna—dinner will be ready in fifteen minutes, okay?" she said.

"Okay," Jenna replied absently, her attention already refocused on the cupid. As her mother walked out of the room, Jenna inched closer to her bureau, examining him intently. "So your name is Max, huh?" she asked.

"That's me," the little cupid said, his huge grin returning. "And you're Jenna. It's a pleasure to meet you," the little cupid said, bending at the waist, twirling his right wrist several times, and extending his hand to her.

Jenna placed her pinky finger in his palm and shook gently. "It's . . . nice to meet you, too," she said, though she was thinking that *weird* was more like it. "But, how did you, you know—*get here*?"

Max shrugged and gave Jenna a bewildered smile. "Actually, I'm not sure," he said. "I've been stuck in your music box for almost seven years now and—"

"But I've only had that music box for six years," Jenna said.

"Yes, but *I* got stuck inside while it was still in the factory."

"How?" Jenna asked.

"I'm not sure exactly," Max said, furrowing his brow. "It all happened so fast—and it was such a long time ago. All I know is that I had just gotten out one of my arrows," he said, patting the pouch on his back that held a bunch of them. "And I was getting ready to shoot, when the conveyor belt I was standing on started moving. It threw me off balance and I fell into a vat of gold paint, and that's all I know. When I came to, I was getting glued onto a pedestal and wired into a music box and there was nothing I could do about it."

"And you've been stuck like that for seven years?" Jenna asked.

"Just about," Max replied. "I tried to get free, but I think the paint I fell into must have been some kind of gold plating or something, because it was really strong. I'd pretty much given up hope of ever flying again, but then today, suddenly *something* snapped me loose."

"What?" Jenna asked.

"I don't know," Max said. "I just felt this . . . tingling on my shoulder, and then I realized I could move it a little, and when you opened the box—poof! I was free!"

"Wait a second—you felt something on your *shoulder*?" Jenna asked, eyeing the bracelet that had fallen onto the bureau when Max broke loose.

"Mm-hmm," Max said with a nod. "A sort of . . . *tingling sensation*. It started in my shoulder and then spread down the length of my arm and into the rest of my body!"

Jenna picked up the bracelet and studied

each of its charms and the shiny silver chain. In the office that afternoon, Amanda had said it was a good luck bracelet, but good luck wasn't the same as magic. Was it?

"It was so bizarre," Max said, his blue eyes wide. "Like I said, I'd been trying to break free for a long time, and then all of a sudden—ping!—I was. I just wish I knew how I did it."

"Maybe *you* didn't," Jenna mumbled, still looking at the bracelet.

"What did you say?" Max asked.

"Nothing," Jenna said. She tucked the bracelet into the front pocket of her light blue roll-up jeans. If it was magic, she wanted to keep it close by. Who knew what else it could do?

Once the bracelet was secured in her pocket, Jenna turned back to the little boy. "So, are you really, like, Cupid? The guy who shoots arrows and makes people fall in love and stuff?"

"Not *the* Cupid," Max said. "One of his assistants—a member of the Noble Order of Cupid," he added proudly. "There are thousands of us, and yes, we really shoot arrows and make people fall in love. It's the noblest job in the world, and now that I'm free, I should be getting back to it. I've got a lot of love and joy to catch up on." Max gave Jenna a big smile and fluttered his wings so that he hovered above the bureau. "It was nice to meet you," he said. "Maybe I'll bump into you again sometime."

Jenna placed her hands on her hips and scowled at the little winged boy. "Wait a second," she said. "You can't just leave."

"Why on Earth not?" Max asked.

"Because—well, what about my music box?"

"Your music box?"

"Yeah, my music box. The one that *used* to have a spinning cupid," Jenna said. "What am I supposed to do now? Just sit here and watch the pedestal turn around and around?"

Max alighted gently on the bureau and gazed at Jenna with sympathetic blue eyes. "It's nice that you're going to miss me, but I'm sure you can find a nice ballerina to spin for you." he suggested. "That would be much more fitting. I was never meant to be in that box in the first place."

"Maybe not," Jenna said, "but you were. And that's why my aunt bought it for me—because of you, because you made it special."

Max glanced at the wooden music box with its gold accents. "It's still nice, even without me," he said. "And you can put anything you want in there—it doesn't have to be a ballerina. Why don't you glue in a dancing alligator? That would be special."

"I don't want a dancing alligator," Jenna said. "I want it back the way it was when my aunt gave it to me—with a spinning, gold cupid."

Max narrowed his eyes. "I'm absolutely not going back on that pedestal!" he said. "I just don't belong there."

"Fine. Wreck my music box!" Jenna retorted, folding her arms across her chest and glaring at him.

"You're being ridiculous," Max said.

Jenna continued to stare. She knew that it was unreasonable to expect Max to stay in the music box, but she didn't think it was right for him to just take off, either.

After a few seconds, Max let out a long sigh and looked up sympathetically at Jenna. "Look," he said. "I'm sorry about your music box, but isn't there something else I can do to make it up to you? Something that doesn't involve gluing myself to that pedestal for another seven years?"

Jenna sighed. What could a two-inch-tall boy with wings, a bow, and a sack full of arrows possibly do for her? *Wait a second . . . arrows?* Suddenly Jenna's eyes lit up. "Do those things really work?" she asked, pointing to Max's pouch.

"My arrows?" Max asked. "Sure, but—"

"Then yes, there *is* something you can do for me," Jenna said with a sly smile. "I have someone I want you to shoot!"

It was about time Noah Carpenter stopped flirting with Keisha and started paying a little more attention to Jenna. If Max could make that happen, she would definitely be willing to forgive him for wrecking her music box.

Max stared down at his feet and shook his head. "I'd love to help you," he said, "but I simply can't."

"What do you mean?" Jenna asked. "You just said the arrows work."

"They do," Max said, "but I can't just go about shooting people willy-nilly. There are rules in this business."

"What kind of rules?"

"Well for one thing, I never shoot anyone under twenty-five years of age. These arrows pack a mighty punch—they aren't for kids."

"That's nice—coming from a two-inch kid!"

"I'm a lot older than you, missy!"

Max pulled an arrow out of his pouch and held it out to Jenna. "See how the feathers and the tip of this arrow are deep red? That means it's the real deal—true love, everlasting. Way too intense for—what are you, a ten-year-old?"

"I'm twelve!" Jenna snapped.

Max shrugged. "Ten, twelve—either way, you're too young. I'm centuries old," he said with a flap of his wings.

Jenna folded her arms and pouted. She hated it when adults gave her that line. And it was especially irritating coming from a chubby, boyish "adult" who was shorter than her toothbrush. "Well what about the green arrows?" she asked, pointing to Max's pouch.

"What green arrows?" Max asked. He turned left and right trying to catch a glimpse of his quiver, but he couldn't quite manage it.

Jenna watched him struggle for a moment, like a dog chasing its own tail. "Hold still!" she told him. Then, carefully, she extracted one of the green arrows from his pack between her fingertips. She passed the arrow to Max, who knit his eyebrows together as he examined it.

"Now how did that get in there?" he muttered. "I shouldn't be carrying any of those."

"There are two more," Jenna said. "What are they for?"

"Training," Max said, running the green feathers through his fingers as he puzzled over the arrow. "New members of NOC—the Noble Order—use them when they're just starting out, but—" Suddenly his eyebrows shot up. "Oh, that's right!" he exclaimed.

"Just before my accident at the music box factory I took one of the newer guys out for some target practice. We must have had a few arrows left over."

"Oh," Jenna said. "And they're magic too, right?"

"Well," Max said, "they're not as powerful as the red ones, and their effects only last a week or two, tops. So you probably wouldn't be interested."

Jenna's eyes lit up. "That's perfect! You can shoot Noah with one of those!"

"But it wouldn't last," Max told her, "regardless of who this Noah is."

"It would last for a week," Jenna said, "and that's long enough for him to forget about Keisha and fall for me instead. He could do that, right? I mean, without another arrow?"

"Oh, sure," Max said. "People fall in love on their own all the time. We just use the arrows to help some of them along."

Jenna raised her eyebrows and smiled. "Excellent," she said. "So you'll shoot Noah, he'll spend a week crushing on me, and by the time the arrow wears off he'll have fallen for me for real."

Max held up one plump index finger. "I hate to ruin this for you," he said, "but I still can't shoot this boy Noah for you. Not even with a training arrow."

"Why not? You said they were less intense."

"They are," Max said. "But I still can't just shoot on demand. I'm only allowed to target people when I get an assignment from the head office. I'd be in big trouble at NOC if anyone found out I was shooting people on my own."

"How would anyone find out?" Jenna barked. "You've been stuck in my music box for seven years. When you show up at the head office, do you really think anyone's going to notice if you're missing a training arrow?"

"Probably not," Max admitted. He took an inspired breath. "But—"

"But nothing," Jenna said. "You asked if there was anything you could do to make up for wrecking my music box, and this is it. So you can either shoot Noah for me, or I can glue you back onto that pedestal—your choice."

Max took a step backward and eyed Jenna from top to bottom. "You're not being very nice," he said, his full lips in full pout mode.

"I don't need to be nice," Jenna said. "You owe me." She folded her arms and held the little cupid's gaze, waiting for him to look away, but he seemed just as determined to maintain eye contact as she was.

"Interesting attitude," Max said. He stood still, silently regarding Jenna as his wings moved steadily forward and back, like a heartbeat. His pout disappeared then and his bright blue eyes became thoughtful. It appeared that he was considering something—Jenna wasn't sure what, but she was getting tired of waiting.

"Well?" she said, tapping her foot impatiently.

Max nodded his head slowly. "I'll shoot the boy," he said. "I think it will be a good lesson for you."

Jenna rolled her eyes. That was the other thing adults were always going on about— learning lessons from everything. "Whatever," she said. All that mattered to her was that Noah would soon forget about Keisha and fall for her—the way it should be.

For that, Jenna would gladly give up the gold, spinning cupid that had adorned her music box for six years now. She was getting a little too old for music boxes anyway.

# CHAPTER
# Four

"Okay. He should be in here," Jenna said, stopping outside of Ms. Garcia's homeroom the next morning. Balancing Max on the notebook she was holding in her arms, she peered through the window in the door. Sure enough, Noah was in there. Unfortunately, so was Keisha.

Jenna clicked her tongue. "Sheesh. Does she always have to hang around him?" she muttered.

"What's wrong?" Max asked.

"Nothing," Jenna said. "Just get ready to shoot. Noah's the one with dark, curly hair. He's wearing a blue-and-white rugby shirt and jeans. Are you ready?"

"Aye aye, captain," Max said with a rigid salute.

"Very funny," Jenna sneered. "Just make sure you get him." With one last firm glance at Max to keep him in line, Jenna opened the door and walked into Ms. Garcia's room. It was only seven fifty-two, so there were still eight minutes before the bell that would send Keisha to her own homeroom.

*Oh well,* Jenna thought. *I guess she'll just have to witness Noah ditching her and falling for me.* It might be awkward, but maybe it would teach her to stay away from guys who were out of her league. *Talk about a good lesson,* Jenna thought. She could hardly wait for Keisha to learn it.

Jenna walked over to where Noah was standing with Keisha and froze. "Ick—what are you doing?" she asked.

Noah turned to her and nodded an informal hello. "Keisha wanted to hold Ziggy," Noah said, referring to the class pet, Ms. Garcia's iguana, "so I'm taking him out for her."

"Oh," Jenna said, trying not to let her lip curl up in disgust as she eyed the foot-long lizard resting on Noah's shoulder. "Cool." She couldn't imagine anyone wanting to hold a scaly, spiky reptile. Jenna didn't even like sitting near his cage during class. All he ever did was lay on his rock and open and close his googly eyes. It was freaky—and not in the least bit cute.

"Do you want to hold him first, Jenna?" Keisha asked with a slight grin.

"*Me?* Um, no, that's okay," Jenna replied. "I

mean, he's our class pet. I can hold him anytime. You go ahead."

"Nice cover," Max said with a smirk. Jenna
scowled at him, and set her notebook down on
her desk so that he could climb off.

"Hey, Jenna, when did you get here?" Emily
asked as she and Sarah approached the group
around Ziggy's tank. In addition to Noah,
Keisha, and Jenna, a couple of Noah's buddies
had come over to see what was going on.

"Yeah. We waited for your bus, but you
weren't on it," Sarah added.

"My mom drove me in this morning," Jenna
said, "so I came in the side door."

"Oh. Well we've been looking all over for
you," Emily said. "We tried to practice the
cheers last night—you know, the ones Becky
and Lindsay showed us yesterday? But neither
one of us could remember how they go."

"We knew you'd have them down, though,"
Sarah gushed. "Do you think maybe you can
help us with them before practice today?"

Jenna squinted at her friends. Couldn't they
do anything on their own? "Before practice?
Like when?"

"I don't know. Lunch?" Emily suggested.

"I'm going to eat lunch during lunch," Jenna
said. "Can't you just practice the cheers at
practice, like everyone else?"

Emily and Sarah exchanged a puzzled look. "I guess," Sarah said.

"It's just that we sort of made a bad first impression yesterday," Emily explained, "so we were kind of hoping to at least look like we have a clue when we show up today."

Out of the corner of her eye, Jenna saw Noah carefully placing the iguana in Keisha's hands and winced. It drove her crazy the way he was always paying so much attention to her. "Yeah, well, I'm sure you'll be fine," she told her friends without bothering to make eye contact. She was still watching Keisha and Noah and about to be sick to her stomach.

"Hey—I think he likes you," Noah said with a flirty smile as Ziggy settled on Keisha's shoulder and snuggled close to her neck.

Keisha giggled, but Jenna frowned. "Maybe you remind him of his rock," she said, turning her head slightly so that only Keisha could see her sarcastic smile. Then she glanced down at the desk where she had set Max to see him staring back up at her, his arms folded across his chest.

"That was a sweet thing to say," he said.

Jenna pressed her lips into a straight line and glared at him. "Just shoot him!" she mouthed nodding toward Noah.

"Is this how you treat everyone, your highness?" Max asked.

"*Now*," Jenna mouthed.

"Fine. But first I have to enchant the arrow," Max said.

Jenna was so irritated that she let a loud sigh escape, causing everyone to turn toward her.

"What's wrong, Jenna?" Emily asked.

"I think I know what it is," Keisha said. With a smirk, she placed a hand on Ziggy, as if to move him. "Jenna wants a chance to hold him," she said with a perfectly straight face.

"Jenna? Hold Ziggy?" Sarah said, starting to giggle.

Emily joined in right away. "Jenna hates rep—"

"I would," Jenna said, "but it's almost time for homeroom, so we have to put him back in his tank."

Noah glanced up at the clock above the dry erase board. "Whoa—she's right," he said. "Here, I'll take him."

As Noah picked up the lizard, Jenna looked down at Max, who appeared to be singing a song to the arrow.

> *Straight and narrow*
> *Magic arrow*
> *With love for Jenna*
> *Fill thy marrow!*

Jenna leaned over, pretending to read something on her notebook cover. "Would you just do it already!" she hissed at the little cupid.

Max scowled at her, but he drew his arrow back in the bow nonetheless. Jenna watched, transfixed, as Max let the arrow fly. It seemed to sail through the air in slow motion. Up, up, up, then arching and coming back down, headed straight for Noah's shoulder. *This is it!* Jenna thought, rubbing her hands together. She grinned down at Max, who was standing on her desk, his bow still in shooting position, and mouthed, "*Thanks.*" The arrow had landed by now, so she walked over to the terrarium where Noah was settling Ziggy onto his warming stone.

"So, Noah," Jenna said, pushing past Keisha with a big smile, "what are you doing this weekend?" Keisha lowered one eyebrow and gazed at Jenna like she was insane, but Jenna took it in stride. Keisha could think whatever she wanted. Noah would be kicking her to the curb —snooty look and all—in a matter of seconds.

"There are a bunch of cool movies out," Jenna went on. "Maybe we could catch one."

Noah turned around and gazed up at Jenna with a bewildered expression. "Are you talking to *me*?" he asked.

Jenna smiled and nodded, waiting for the distant look in Noah's eyes to melt into a mixture of awe and adoration, but instead he just stared at her. She glanced back at Max, who was still on her desk, and widened her eyes with urgency.

"Be patient," the little cupid said. "Sometimes it takes a minute to kick in." Jenna frowned. She'd expected immediate results. That's the way these kinds of things always worked in movies and on TV. But, if she had to wait a moment or two for the magic to kick in, she could wait. Having Noah in love with her—and Keisha out of the way—was well worth a few more minutes of her time.

She turned back to Noah, who was tending to Ziggy again. "Yeah," she said. "I was just saying that there are some cool movies coming out this week and I thought maybe—"

"Ziggy!" Noah called suddenly, and before Jenna knew what was going on, the iguana had climbed up Noah's arm and out of his terrarium, leaping onto the floor.

"Quick! Catch him!" Keisha cried. She squatted down and tried to grab the lizard, but he was too fast for her. The other kids in the room began chasing the lizard around as well, but nobody was able to catch him.

Amid the chaos, Ms. Garcia ran over and closed the door so Ziggy wouldn't escape into the hallway. "All right, everyone!" she called out over all the noise. "Calm down and stand in one place."

Remarkably, everyone listened and stood still

as the lizard sprinted across the floor on his hind legs. Jenna squirmed, wishing she could jump up on a chair to avoid him, but she knew everyone would laugh if she did, so instead, she just watched as the little green blur sped around the room. Then suddenly, as quickly as he had bolted in the first place, the lizard stopped, right at Jenna's feet, and gazed upward.

"Don't move, Jenna," Ms. Garcia said, slowly making her way toward the lizard. It was a difficult command to obey. More than anything Jenna wanted to scream and run out of the room, but she did her best to keep it together. As Ms. Garcia approached, Jenna stood frozen to the floor.

"Ziggy, hold still," Ms. Garcia said, trying to cup the iguana in her hands, and for a second it looked like she had him. But before Ms. Garcia could get a good grip, Ziggy wriggled free.

"Where did he—?" Jenna started, but the sensation of iguana claws making their way up the front of her embroidered pink bell-bottomed jeans shocked her into silence. She stared down in horror at the small green reptile climbing her thigh. "S-someone g-get him!" she stammered. And then, just when she thought there was no way things could get any worse, they did.

Jenna's eyes widened in shock as she realized what had happened. The arrow hadn't hit Noah! It had landed smack in the middle of Ziggy's forehead, right in between his two googly eyes. And now he was staring up at her with a mixed expression of awe and longing.

"It's okay, Jenna," Ms. Garcia said. The arrow must have been invisible to the others, too. "Just hold still. I'll get him." She made another grab for the lizard, but Ziggy leaped—from Jenna's leg to her arm—and continued his ascent.

Jenna let out a piercing scream and began waving her arms in the air. "Get him off! Get him off!" she shouted. But Ziggy dug in with his claws and held his position on her shoulder, where he sat staring up at Jenna lovingly. He didn't seem the least bit bothered by her flailing, but Jenna didn't find his patience endearing. "Get this slimy thing off of me!" she shouted again.

"Stop screaming!" Noah ordered as he ran over to help Ms. Garcia capture the iguana. "And stop trying to hit him—you're going to hurt him!"

"I'm not trying to hit him! I don't even want to touch him! Just get him—" Jenna stopped mid-rant, stunned into silence by a scaly tail flicking in front of her face and slapping her nose and cheeks. The iguana had jumped onto her head.

Jenna blinked a few times and tried to speak. "A-ba, a-ba, a-ba," she sputtered at first, and then, finding her voice, she let out a piercing scream. And another . . . and another. She was so distressed by the situation that all she could do was stand rooted to the floor shrieking.

Ziggy held on to her long, dark hair with remarkable skill. She could feel him sliding around on her head, scrambling to stay on top, but it seemed like nothing would dislodge him.

Finally, after what felt like an eternity, Jenna felt the lizard being lifted off. Bringing both hands to her chest, she willed herself to take a few deep breaths in order to calm her pounding heart. "Oh. My. Gosh," she said, still panting. "That was horrible. It was . . ." Jenna's voice trailed off as another sound filled her ears—laughter.

She'd been so freaked out by the iguana on her head that she'd completely forgotten about the other kids in the room. They were all laughing at her: Keisha; Emily; Sarah; *Max, that little runt*; Noah's buddies, Justin and Luke; and five or six others who had filed into Ms. Garcia's class for homeroom. Even Ms. Garcia was chuckling, although she had a hand over her mouth in an attempt to hide her amusement.

Jenna felt her cheeks burn red. *Everyone* was laughing at her. Everyone, that was, except Noah, who was carefully placing Ziggy back in his terrarium.

"Are you all right, Jenna?" asked Ms. Garcia, who was the first to regain her composure.

"I'm fine," Jenna snapped. *Just what did they all think was so funny, anyway?* She glared down at Max, who was pressing his lips together and trying not to smile.

"Here, Jenna," Sarah said, brushing a strand of hair off of Jenna's cheek. Jenna shoved her friend's hand away. "Geez! I'm just trying to help!" Sarah said. "Your hair's all messed up."

"Yeah, Ziggy kind of gave you a new 'do," Emily added with a grin.

"It looks great," Keisha joked. "Maybe you should stop by Ziggy's tank every morning." Emily and Sarah giggled, and so did the two or three other kids who were still standing around.

Jenna glared at Max. This was all his fault.

"Sorry," he said with a shrug. "I guess I'm a little rusty."

"Obviously," Jenna sneered.

"Obviously what?" Keisha asked.

Jenna glanced over at Keisha, surprised. She knew she shouldn't speak to Max aloud, but she hadn't realized anyone was listening. They had all seemed so preoccupied with making fun of her. "Obviously *you* have a big mouth," she told Keisha, making sure that everyone heard her this time.

There was a collective "oohhhh" from the small group around her, but Jenna ignored them and went straight over to Ms. Garcia's desk to ask for the bathroom pass.

"Take your time," Ms. Garcia said sympathetically.

She started out of the classroom. When she passed Ziggy's tank, where Noah was still kneeling, the iguana rushed over and tried to scrabble up the glass to get to her. Noah, on the other hand, didn't even glance in her direction.

*Wonderful,* Jenna thought, lifting her notebook—and Max—into her arms. *Noah can't stand me, but the lizard's in love.* When she was out in the hallway, she gave the little cupid one last glare. "You have two training arrows left," she told him, "and the next one better hit Noah or you're going back in the music box for good."

When she entered the gym that afternoon, Jenna walked straight to the bleachers and set her messenger bag—with Max in the front pocket— at one end, far away from everyone else.

"Stay right here," she told the little cupid,

"and do some target practice, will you? I don't need anymore reptile boyfriends, okay?"

"I—" Max started, but Jenna ignored him. She didn't want to hear more of his lame excuses. So what if he'd been encased in gold for the last seven years? He worked for Cupid. He shot arrows. That was his job. *And he better get good at it fast if he ever wants to get back to it,* Jenna thought.

Purposefully, she strode toward the group of girls standing in the center of the gym. "Hi, Becky. Hi, Lindsay," she said, gluing a smile onto her face. She gave a vivacious wave to the other eighth graders, and they all waved back. Jenna knew that if she wanted to be a cheerleader she needed to look happy—even when her best boyfriend prospect was four-legged and green.

"Hi, Jenna," Becky said. Then she raised her eyebrows at Lindsay expectantly.

Lindsay smirked and then said, "Are your . . . *friends* coming back today?"

Jenna shifted her weight to her left foot and tilted her head. She was pretty sure she knew who they were talking about but it was best to play dumb. "What friends?" she asked.

"You know," Becky said, "those two sixth graders who came in late yesterday. What are their names?"

"Emily and Sarah," Lindsay answered.

"Right—them," Becky said with a nod. "Aren't they like, your best friends or something?" Jenna hesitated, uncertain how to answer. "I mean, you hang around with them in school all the time, don't you?"

Jenna looked at Becky, Lindsay, and the other three eighth graders gathered in the gym. No one else had arrived yet. "Well, I wouldn't call them my *best* friends," Jenna said, even though she really hadn't hung out with anyone else since the beginning of the school year.

"Then how come you're always with them?" Lindsay asked.

Again Jenna glanced around the gym. Other girls were trickling in now, but there was still no sign of Emily and Sarah. They'd probably be late again today. Jenna couldn't afford to be associated with them—at least, not while she was trying to make the cheerleading team. "Actually, it's more like *they're* always with *me*," she said. "I mean, they're nice and everything, but they follow me *everywhere*. It's like they can't do anything on their own."

Becky gave Lindsay a smug smile. "See?" she said. "I told you Jenna was too cool for them."

Lindsay tilted her head and gave a half shrug.

"I guess," she said. "Hey—it's two-thirty. We better get started. I'm meeting Theo at four and I don't want to be late." Theo was Lindsay's boyfriend—a ninth grader who she'd been seeing off and on since he was in eighth grade at Adams and she was in seventh. Now he went to Anderson, a local private high school, and Lindsay liked to drop his name into conversations whenever she could. She knew that having a high-school boyfriend made her twice as cool as she already was to most of her peers.

"Okay everybody!" Becky yelled. "Let's get in a big circle and stretch out!"

Instantly, all of the girls in the gym—including Emily and Sarah, who had just entered— flocked to the middle of the floor and made a big circle around Becky and Lindsay, who were, of course, leading the stretches.

Jenna strategically positioned herself next to Andrea Killiard and Molly O'Connell again, and avoided making eye contact with Sarah and Emily. She avoided Michelle Burton and Lucy Greene, too, knowing that it was best to separate herself from all of the sixth graders, just to be safe.

Becky and Lindsay led the rest of the girls through a bunch of yoga postures, including a series called "Salute the Sun" that Jenna really liked. Apparently Becky's mother was a yoga instructor who had helped out with the team last year and was planning to help again this year once the squad was chosen.

"Our coach, Ms. Fine, has us do yoga for warm-up and cool-down every day," Becky said. "She says it helps with focus and balance, so if you make the team you can plan on doing a lot of it."

*Cool,* Jenna thought. She'd been wanting to try yoga for a while, and now it looked like she'd be getting free lessons—as long as she made the team. *And I should,* Jenna thought. Then again, she'd thought she was a shoo-in for student council and that twit Amanda Littlefield had beaten her. But this was different. This was cheerleading, and Jenna had what it took to make the squad: She was popular, the older girls thought she was cool, and she was super coordinated. She'd never done yoga before, but thanks to her experience with gymnastics and dance it came fairly easily to her, as did the cheers. Sarah and Emily on the other hand ...

Jenna snuck a look across the circle at her two friends. They were doing their best to follow Becky and Lindsay as they moved from Triangle Pose into Warrior II, but their feet were way out of position and their arms looked like they'd been taken off and put on backward. With a quick glance to the right, Jenna saw that Michelle and Lucy were in the same boat. It was obvious that none of them had ever done yoga before—or dance or gymnastics or anything that might help them to pick it up quickly.

*If someone would just show them how to change their foot position,* Jenna thought, *they'd be in much better shape.* But no one was offering to help them. In fact, it looked like Becky, Lindsay, and some of the other girls who were already on the squad were actually laughing at them.

"Check it out," Jenna heard Lindsay mutter, stifling a giggle.

Becky glanced over her shoulder at Sarah and Emily, then turned back to Lindsay with a snort. Then she mouthed, "More behind you." Lindsay pretended to be stretching out her neck as she turned to observe Michelle and Lucy, then looked at Becky and chortled. Some of the other squad members caught on to the joke and started giggling at the four clueless sixth graders as well.

Jenna watched, realizing that while there were some pretty uncoordinated seventh graders, too, they weren't drawing nearly as much attention as Emily, Sarah, Michelle, and Lucy. Probably because they were tight with some of the eighth grade girls, which put them beyond ridicule.

She glanced at her friends again. It was too bad that no one was helping them with their postures. More than once, Jenna considered pointing out what they could do differently, but if she did, she knew that she could become the next target, and that was something she wasn't willing to risk. So instead, she just watched carefully and made sure that she hit all of her poses perfectly. As long as she laid low, Jenna was pretty sure she'd get picked for the team. There was no reason to put herself in the spotlight unless it was to be praised for doing something well.

After practice, when Jenna had finished chatting with Molly, Andrea, Becky, Lindsay, and a few of the other popular girls, she went over to the bleachers to collect Max and her things.

"Hop in," she told the cupid, holding out the front pocket on her bag. Max gazed up at her for a moment and then just folded his arms and looked away.

"What's your problem?" Jenna asked him, but Max remained silent. "Okay, look," Jenna huffed, "I don't have time for this. My mom's probably waiting outside right now. Would you just get in the bag?" When Max still refused to budge, Jenna added a scornful, "*Please?*"

Slowly, Max turned to face her, his blue eyes narrowed and his usually grinning mouth curved into a sneer. "You disgust me!" he blurted.

"What?" Jenna demanded.

"Those girls are your friends," Max said.

"Who?"

"Emily and Sarah," Max replied.

"Oh, them," Jenna scoffed. "So?"

"So you treated them like dirt!"

"I did not!"

"Really?" Max asked. "Look—I may be small, but I have good ears."

"You should," Jenna said. "They're about five times too big for your head." Five times was certainly an exaggeration, but underneath his curly blonde hair, the cupid did have rather large ears—cute, but for his chubby, round face, a bit large.

Max stared at her, his mouth hanging open. "You're truly unbelievable!" he said, shaking his head. "The point is, I heard you sell them out at the beginning of practice, and then I watched you just stand there through the rest of it while people made fun of them."

"I didn't do that," Jenna said, even though part of her knew that Max was right. But what did he expect her to do? Tell Becky and Lindsay she didn't think they were being nice? Yeah, right. That would make her look really cool. *Not.*

"Yes, you did!" Max said, "I sat right here and watched you. And you didn't even try to help them learn the cheers—nobody did. What kind of team is this?"

"A *good* one," Jenna said. "One that doesn't want a bunch of uncoordinated cheerleaders who can't tell their right foot from their left arm."

"Is that what you think of your friends? That they're just uncoordinated oafs? Don't you like them? Don't you enjoy their company? Aren't they important to you?"

Jenna sighed. "Look, I'm just tired of them always hanging around me and depending on me to make them popular and help them meet cool people and make the cheerleading team and everything. They're just so . . . *immature.*"

"I'm not sure they're the ones with the maturity problem," Max replied. "They're acting their age. You're the one who's trying to be something you aren't."

"I am not!" Jenna proclaimed. "How can you say that? You've only known me for one day. And this is none of your business anyway."

Max took a moment to gaze at Jenna. He was looking deep into her eyes, as though he was searching for something, and Jenna didn't like it. She turned away.

"I want you to take this," Max said. Jenna glanced over her shoulder to see him removing something from a pouch that was attached to the strap of his quiver, which ran diagonally across his body.

He held his hand out to her, and Jenna squatted down, looking at a tiny pink pebble in his hand. "What is *that*?" she asked.

"It's rose quartz," Max replied. "I always keep some handy so I can put it down where people who need it can find it. But *you*," he went on, shaking his head. "I'm not sure you'd find it if I glued it to your forehead."

"What's *that* supposed to mean?" Jenna snarled.

"Let's just say, you're not very open to love," Max told her.

Jenna rolled her eyes. What kind of baloney was he trying to give her now? "Max, we have to get going."

"See what I mean?" Max said. "You don't even like hearing the word. *Love*," he repeated, fluttering his wings and rising until he was right next to Jenna's ear. "Love, love, love, love, love."

Jenna exhaled heavily. "Would you quit it?" she said, swatting at him as if he were a mosquito, but Max was undeterred.

"*Looooove*," he sang out at the top of his voice, "is a many splendored thing! It's the April rose that only grows in early spring! Love is nature's way of—"

"All right, fine," Jenna said, slumping down on the bleachers. "Give me the silly rock." Slowly, Max landed next to her and held out his palm. Jenna snatched it up and looked it over. "What do you want me to do with it?"

"Just hold onto it," Max said. "Put it in your pocket or something and carry it everywhere you go. Every time you touch it, it will help to fill your heart with love." As he said these last words, he brought his hands to his chest and batted his wings and eyelashes dramatically.

Jenna gave the little winged boy a sideways glance. *Great*. Not only was this cupid a bad shot, he was insane. "Max, I don't think—"

"Do you want me to shoot Noah with one of these arrows?" he asked, pointing to his quiver.

"Yes, but—"

"Then carry the stone," Max said. "And try to imagine how you would feel if you were the one who couldn't figure out the cheer and no one would help you."

Jenna snorted. The little archer didn't know what he was talking about. She'd never put herself in that position.

"Just try, okay?" Max said. "Rose quartz is also called 'love stone,' and lots of people carry a piece with them to remind them to be kind and patient. That's all I'm asking you to do."

"Fine," Jenna said. "I'll do it if it will get you in this pocket."

"I can't wait!" Max called as he took a flying leap that landed him right in the front of Jenna's messenger bag. As Jenna hefted the bag onto her shoulder and started out of the gym, Max popped his head back out of the pocket and said, "I think you'll find that carrying the stone will make you look at things quite differently."

Jenna shook her head. "Whatever."

"Hmph," Max replied, and returned to the pocket.

*Let the little cupid think what he wants,* she thought. *He just better pray that his next arrow hits its mark.*

# CHAPTER
## Five

"Okay, arrow boy," Jenna said the next morning as she closed her locker door. "This is it—your second chance—and you better get it right."

Max scowled. "Are you carrying your love stone?" he asked. "I don't sense any love here."

"Yes, I have your ridiculous *rock*," Jenna said, barely moving her lips. It was seven-forty, and the hall was crowded with students who still had twenty minutes to kill before they needed to be in homeroom. It was loud, so Jenna wasn't worried about anyone overhearing her, but she was concerned that someone might *see* her. It had been bad enough being laughed at when the iguana was on her head. She didn't need people joking about how she'd started talking to herself.

"Where is it?" Max asked.

"In my pocket," Jenna said.

Max eyed Jenna's outfit—a cranberry-colored, pleated miniskirt with front and back pockets, and a crisp white top with small pockets on each sleeve and one at the bottom of the front right side. "Which one?" he asked.

Jenna groaned and dug the stone out of one of the miniskirt's front pockets. "It's right here, okay?"

"Good," Max said, eyeing the small, translucent pink gem. "Hold onto it and remember, every time you touch it, it will help you to be patient, kind, and open to love."

"Yeah, yeah," Jenna said, returning the rock to her pocket. "I'll be patient when your aim improves."

"Jenna, you need to find some compassion in your heart," Max said. "You can't keep treating people like they're your personal servants and expect them to—"

"Shh!" Jenna hissed. "I hear Noah. He must be in Ms. Garcia's room. I hope he's not holding that stinky lizard again," she mumbled as she and Max, who was peeking out of the side of her bag, rounded the corner and walked into Ms. Garcia's room.

Ziggy immediately perked up and ran over to the side of his terrarium closest to Jenna, scratching at the glass. "Gross," Jenna muttered, eyeing the iguana. His creepy eyes were trained on her and it made her skin crawl.

"Someone's happy to see you," Max said, stifling a chuckle. "But that'll wear off in a week—maybe faster, the way *you* treat people."

Jenna scowled at the little cupid and glanced around the room. There were a few boys playing a computer game in the back, but no Noah. "I swear I heard him," she muttered, letting Max climb onto her palm. "Let's check the hall again."

As soon as Jenna exited Ms. Garcia's room, she heard Noah's voice. It was coming from across the hall—from Mrs. MacKnight's room. *What's he doing in there?* she wondered. Then she grimaced. Keisha was in Mrs. MacKnight's homeroom. Sure enough, when Jenna peered through the doorway she saw Noah sitting at the front of the room with Keisha, her two friends Amanda and Sam, and his buddies Justin and Luke. And they were all eating muffins from a platter on Mrs. MacKnight's desk.

"Darn it!" Jenna muttered, backing away and flattening herself against the wall. "Are they attached at the hip?"

"Well, he certainly likes her," Max said simply.

"Thank you!" Jenna barked. "But why? She's

not pretty, she's not popular, and she's not part of our crowd. I mean, look who she hangs around with—the two biggest freaks in the school, Amanda Littlefield and Sam Sullivan. Why does he want anything to do with her?"

Max shook his head. "Love—in all of its forms—has very little to do with what's on the surface," he told Jenna. "It's more about what's underneath." He patted his heart with his hand. "That's where real beauty is, and that's where real love is, too." He fluttered his wings as he spoke. He had a goofy grin on his face, and at the same time Jenna noticed that it looked like his eyes were beginning to tear up.

*Please!* Jenna thought. She gave the little cupid a sideways glance. "Put it in a greeting card," she sneered, "and stop boring me with your little pearls of wisdom. I don't need your advice. I just need you to get in there and shoot Noah like you were supposed to do yesterday."

Max's watery eyes dried up as he scowled up at her. "But Jenna, if you don't—"

"If I don't what? Glue you back into my music box for breaking your promise to me? You said you'd shoot Noah for me, and that's what I want you to do. Now go!" she finished, setting Max on the floor and giving him a little push.

He stood there staring up at her for a moment, his arms folded and his head cocked to one side. "You're really bossy, you know that?"

"*Just go*," Jenna mouthed, and with one more disgusted look in her direction, the little cupid rounded the door frame and set off on his mission. Jenna pulled a nail file from her bag and stood nonchalantly against the white cinder block wall, cleaning and shaping her fingernails.

From inside Mrs. MacKnight's room she heard laughter interspersed with Max's chanting.

> *Magic arrow*
> *When thou dost fly*
> *Bring love for Jenna*
> *To thy target's eye!*

Listening carefully, Jenna was able to hear the twang of Max's bow, and a few seconds later, the little cupid reappeared outside the door.

"Did you do it?" Jenna asked.

"Yes."

"And did you hit him?"

"I think so," Max said, rubbing at his eye.

"*You think so?*" Jenna demanded, squatting down to get a better look at the tiny cupid.

"I'm pretty sure I did," Max said, "but it was hard to see. They're eating muffins, you know, and a crumb flew into my eye just as I was letting the arrow go."

"Are you kidding me?" Jenna asked.

"Hey—I'm doing the best I can," Max replied. "Now please—get me some water so I can flush my eye out?"

"Just keep it closed. It'll water on its own," Jenna told him, scooping him up and perching him on her shoulder. Then she started into the room.

All eyes turned as Jenna entered, and all of them, save Mrs. MacKnight's, looked surprised—and not exactly happy—to see her.

"Would you like a muffin, Miss Scott?" the teacher asked, holding out a silver platter. "Fresh baked this morning at my house," she added in a grandmotherly tone.

"Sure," Jenna said, putting on the smile she usually saved for meeting her parents' important friends. "Thank you, Mrs. MacKnight." She took a muffin from the tray even though she wasn't hungry and went to sit down next to Noah and the others. "So—what's going on?" she asked brightly.

Everyone around the table stared at her with narrowed eyes and furrowed brows. *What's their problem?* Jenna wondered. True, she'd never actually hung out with Amanda, Sam, or Keisha . . . or even really talked to them unless she was teasing them or making fun of them in some way. But she hadn't been particularly mean to them in the last couple of weeks, and she was being nice now. Couldn't they put the past behind them and do the same?

Then again, even if Sam, Amanda, and Keisha couldn't get past their history with Jenna, there was no reason for Justin, Luke, and Noah to act so surprised to see her. She'd hung out with all of them before. At least, she'd hung out with Noah, and Justin and Luke were his best friends, so sometimes they'd been around when she was talking to him. *And I must have talked to them, too,* Jenna thought, although she wasn't completely sure of it.

"Good muffins, huh?" she said. But instead of agreeing, everyone continued to stare at her like she was a stranger who'd just walked into a family picnic. Jenna was beginning to feel uneasy when Sam finally spoke up.

"Yeah," he said. "They are. Thanks again, Mrs. MacKnight," he called over Jenna's shoulder.

Mrs. MacKnight smiled. "Tomorrow I'm making chocolate chip," she said. "You'll have to make sure you come back."

"Definitely," Jenna gushed, and once again there was silence around the table. Not even Noah—*who was supposed to be falling in love with her*—looked happy to see her.

"Did you . . . *want* something, Jenna?" Amanda asked.

"Huh? Oh," Jenna stammered. For the first time since she was five and her mother had made her sit on Santa Claus's lap at the mall, Jenna felt extremely uncomfortable and out of place. "I, um, just wanted to check and make sure that Ziggy was all right," she said, glancing at Noah. "I mean, you know, after what happened yesterday."

Noah scowled in Jenna's general direction but didn't say anything, so Jenna, feeling more uncomfortable by the minute, continued to babble. "I don't know what got into me. I usually love holding iguanas and . . . things. I guess it was just the way he climbed up my leg and right onto my head, you know? I mean, it was kind of weird, don't you think?"

"It was kind of funny, actually," Keisha said. "You should have seen your face. She was totally freaked out," she told Amanda and Sam. Then Keisha did an impression of Jenna with the lizard on her head, screaming, "Get it off! Get it off!" and sending everyone in the room into peels of laughter.

"I wish I'd been there for that," Amanda said, chuckling.

"Yeah, well," Jenna said, failing to see the humor in the situation. "Anyway, I just wanted to make sure he was all right." Again, she gazed at Noah, hoping to see a glimmer of attraction in his eyes, but there was nothing.

"Why don't you go check?" he suggested, his expression flat. "He's in his terrarium in Ms. Garcia's room, right where he always is."

"That's a good idea," Jenna said. "Let's go."

Noah squinted at Jenna like she'd just suggested he jump off a cliff, then he turned to Justin and Luke. "We still have ten minutes. You guys want to see if we can shoot some hoops before the bell?"

"Sure," Justin and Luke replied, and the three of them stood up to leave.

"Thanks for getting Mr. Fluffy out," Noah said to Keisha, with a smile.

Keisha grinned back. "No problem," she said. "He definitely likes you," she added, blinking up at Noah coyly. Noah shot her his incredibly cute crooked smile as he left the room and Jenna felt her stomach lurch. *He should be looking at* me *that way. Not her,* she thought, but Noah had barely looked at her at all.

She glared down at Max who shrugged and said, "I don't get it. I shot straight at him. I don't know where it could have—" He stopped suddenly, staring at the tank behind the chair where Noah had been sitting. Inside the tank was Mr. Fluffy, a guinea pig who was the class pet for Mrs. MacKnight's homeroom. And in the wood shavings, right next to Mr. Fluffy, was a tiny arrow with green feathers.

*I don't believe this*, Jenna thought, glowering at the little archer. How could he have missed again?

"Oops," Max said quietly.

Abruptly, Jenna stood up from the table. "I have to get going, too," she said.

"Are you going to check on Ziggy?" Keisha asked, an edge of sarcasm in her voice. "I know how much you love iguanas." Both Sam and Amanda smirked.

"Very funny," Jenna sneered. There was no need to keep up the pretense now that Noah was gone. And there was definitely no reason to stay without him here, either. As she turned to leave the room, Mr. Fluffy looked up from his food bowl, noticing her for the first time. Suddenly, his large, brown guinea pig eyes seemed to widen, and his nose began to twitch madly. He hopped closer to the glass and pressed his face against it, staring longingly at Jenna.

*Wonderful*, Jenna thought as she strode out of the room. Every animal at Adams Middle School was going to be in love with her before Noah Carpenter would even give her the time of day.

# CHAPTER
## Six

"Hey Jenna—you know that part in the second cheer when we say, 'but when you're playing Adams / tough is not enough'?" Sarah asked.

"It's 'when you're up against the Falcons,'" Jenna replied. "Not 'when you're playing Adams.'"

"Yeah, that part," Sarah said.

"What about it?" Jenna asked absently. It was break time—the twenty-minute interval between period two and period three that had recently been added to the middle school schedule—and she, Emily, and Sarah were hanging out at their lockers. Jenna was resting against hers with one leg bent so that her knee jutted out in front of her, and she was only half listening to her friends' questions about cheering.

"What are we supposed to do with our arms when we say that?" Emily asked. "I always get mine mixed up."

"It's up, out, side, side, down," Jenna answered, glancing just over her friends' heads.

"What?" Emily and Sarah asked at the same time.

"Like this," Jenna said, quickly demonstrating the arm movements. Then she peered over her friends' heads again.

A little ways down the hall she could see Noah getting his basketball sneakers out of his locker, which meant he'd be coming her way soon. He had to go past her locker to get to the gym, and when he did, she was going to be ready. Or rather, Max was.

He was already stationed up on top of the lockers so that he had a good vantage point from which to target Noah. Jenna had set him up there at the beginning of break and given him strict orders to be ready to shoot at all times.

She glanced up at him now and nodded subtly in Noah's direction. "I see him, I see him," Max said. "And believe me—I'll get him this time, too. I'm beginning to think that your attitude is never going to change, and I've had just about all I can take of it."

Jenna frowned at the little archer and turned back to her friends, who were staring at her expectantly. "What?" she asked.

Emily sighed. "Haven't you been listening to us at all?"

"Of course I have," Jenna lied.

"Well? What do you think?" Sarah asked.

Jenna wrinkled her nose and looked back and forth between her two friends. "It depends," she tried.

"On what?" Emily asked.

*Busted,* Jenna thought. "On what you asked," she replied.

This time, both Emily *and* Sarah exhaled heavily. "Honestly, Jenna," Emily said. "What's going on with you lately? You've been acting really strange around us. Is it because of cheering? Are you mad that we're trying out for the team?"

Jenna snorted. "Why would I care?"

Sarah and Emily looked at each other and shook their heads. "I don't know," Sarah said, "but Emily's right. You've been acting different ever since tryouts started."

Jenna rolled her eyes and gazed back down the hall toward Noah. He would be coming their way any minute. Did they really have to get into this right now?

"Yeah, you've been acting even ruder than usual," Emily said, stepping right in front of Jenna so that she couldn't avoid eye contact.

Jenna sighed. "Talk about rude," she said. "What do you call that?"

"Sor-ry," Emily said. "But you've been treating us like dirt, and we're getting tired of it."

*That's insane,* Jenna thought, lowering one eyebrow and gazing at her friends. *I'm treating them like dirt? They're lucky to be hanging around with me in the first place.* "Get over yourselves," she told them. "Just because I'm not spending every minute of my day helping you learn the cheers, it doesn't mean that I'm being rude. You're supposed to learn them on your own, if you haven't noticed—that's what the rest of us are doing. And if you can't, then maybe you don't belong on the team."

Emily's mouth dropped open, and Sarah was gaping at Jenna with eyes the size of basketballs.

"I don't believe you!" Emily exclaimed. She started to say something else, but Jenna had stopped listening. Out of the corner of her eye she'd spotted Noah coming down the hall and she didn't want Max to miss this time.

Turning her head away from her friends, she saw Max placing his last green arrow in his bow. "I've got this covered," he told her. "You'd better focus on your friends or they won't *be* your friends much longer."

"Jenna—are you listening to me?" Emily

shouted. Jenna whirled around and stared at her for a moment, but when she heard Max enchanting the arrow, she had to look away. She had to see what was going to happen.

*Last green arrow in my possession*
*Jenna Scott make thy obsession*
*And fill thy target's heart with love*
*When I shoot him from above!*

Jenna watched Noah approaching, vaguely aware that Emily was still yelling at her, and then she heard the *twang!* of Max's arrow as he released it. Continuing to ignore her ranting friends, Jenna watched the arrow's flight as it ricocheted off the ceiling, hit the opposite wall, bounced back and headed straight for Jenna.

Suddenly, with ninja-like reflexes that Jenna never would have guessed he possessed, Max leaped off the locker and onto Jenna's shoulder. Just in time he gave the arrow a kick that sent it back toward Noah, spinning end over end. Jenna watched in anticipation, her heart pounding inside her chest, and listened, as an imaginary sports announcer in her heard called out, "It's going, going. . ." And then suddenly, it was gone! The arrow whirred past Noah's left ear, grazed his hair, and disappeared.

*Nooooooo!* Jenna watched as Noah passed without so much as a glance in her direction.

She turned to glare at Max, who was covering his wide-open mouth with one hand, then stormed across the hall to retrieve the errant arrow. Jenna had no idea where it had landed, but she was guessing it had ended up on the floor, and if that was the case, she was getting it back. She wasn't going to give up her last chance to enchant Noah easily.

"Jenna!" Emily shouted after her as she walked away, but Jenna didn't stop. If she didn't find the arrow quickly, someone might step on it and break it. And who knew if it would still work then?

She was just about to kneel down and start searching the floor when a glimmer of green caught her eye. Jenna turned and spotted the arrow, utterly shocked at where she saw it had landed.

"Give me that!" she cried, snatching the fishbowl from Sam Sullivan's arms.

"Jenna?" he said, staring at her in disbelief, his deep red eyebrows knit together. Jenna ignored him and plunged her hand into the fishbowl, sending water splashing over the sides. "What are you doing? You're making a mess!" Sam exclaimed, but Jenna didn't care. She sifted through the red pebbles at the bottom of the bowl and retrieved Max's arrow.

"Hah!" she cried, pulling her hand out triumphantly. Swiftly, she tucked the arrow into the pocket on the front of her shirt and thrust the bowl back at Sam. "Here," she said. Then a thought occurred to her. She scanned the bowl, seeing nothing but water, pebbles, and a tiny plastic treasure chest. "Where's the fish?" she asked.

Sam glared at her with what seemed to be a mixture of confusion and concern. "In Mr. Hupp's room," he answered slowly. "In a mug of water. I'm taking the bowl to the teacher's room to clean it out."

"Phew," Jenna breathed, stepping back across the hall. The last thing she needed was to have Fido, Mr. Hupp's fish, pining after her during math class and making kissy faces.

When she'd returned to her locker, Jenna noticed that not only was Sam staring at her, but so were Sarah, Emily, and several other students who had witnessed the scene she'd just made with the fishbowl. "What?" she sneered, glaring at them all.

Sam shot her one last bewildered glance and continued on toward the teachers' room, while the other students who'd been watching just giggled and turned away. Sarah and Emily, however, were staring at her like she'd just sprouted antlers and a tail.

"Are you . . . *okay*?" Sarah asked. From her tone, Jenna could tell that Sarah had already determined the answer to her question: definitely not. But that didn't stop Jenna from answering to the contrary.

"I'm fine," she said. "Why?"

Sarah and Emily looked her up and down like they were trying to make sense of a particularly baffling puzzle. "Because you're acting like a freak," Emily answered.

"Nice," Jenna said, rolling her eyes. "Look, I don't have time for this. I don't need to stand here and be insulted by people who are supposed to be my friends. I have better things to do." Without another glance at Sarah or Emily she plucked Max off the top of her locker, slung her messenger bag over her shoulder, and stalked off.

"Don't you think you were a bit brash with your friends?" Max demanded once Jenna had turned the corner into a less populated corridor.

"*So?*" Jenna replied. "They'll get over it."

"I'm not so sure about that," Max replied.

"Trust me, they will," Jenna said. "They always do. But," she added, removing the green arrow from her pocket and passing it to him, "if you miss a fourth time, I won't."

# CHAPTER
## Seven

At lunch, when Jenna entered the cafeteria, Max, who was fluttering in the air by her ear, spotted Sarah and Emily right away. "Look," he said, "they're already sitting down at your regular table. Don't they usually wait for you?"

Jenna glanced over and saw her two friends. It was odd for them to sit down without even checking in with her, but neither one of them had even tried to talk to her since break. *They're probably still upset that they can't figure out the cheers on their own,* she thought. But that wasn't her problem.

She watched them from the lunch line for a moment, and at least once she was positive that Emily had spotted her. But instead of waving like she normally would have, Emily had just looked away and whispered something to Sarah. Jenna had the distinct feeling that they were talking about her. A heavy feeling stirred in the pit of her stomach, but she pushed it away. *Hmph. Fine*, she thought. *Let them be that way*.

She turned to Max, who was eyeing her suspiciously. "I wasn't planning to sit with them today anyway," she told him. It wasn't entirely true, but that didn't matter. She had other friends to sit with. Who needed Sarah and Emily?

After making her way through the line and picking up a yogurt and a tossed salad along with an order of fries and a soda, Jenna headed for the table where Lindsay, Becky, and some of the other members of the cheerleading squad were sitting.

"Hey, Jenna," Becky said, obviously pleased to see her. "Grab a seat. I was hoping I'd get a chance to talk with you before practice today."

"Really? What's up?" Jenna asked, sitting down on a vacant stool a few seats down.

Becky leaned over the table and spoke in a hushed tone. "I just thought you'd want to know—you're definitely going to make the squad."

Jenna's face lit up. "Really?" she asked, her eyebrows shooting upward. She knew she was as good a cheerleader as anyone else who was trying out, including the eighth graders who were already on the team, but as confident as she was in her ability, she'd been worried that being a sixth grader might still hold her back. Especially if she was seen as a package-deal with Emily and Sarah.

"Yes, *really*," Becky said with a grin.

"Aren't tryouts still a week away?" Max asked from his perch on top of Jenna's unopened strawberry yogurt.

Hearing him, Jenna lowered her eyebrows and squinted at Becky. "But tryouts are still a week away. How do you know I'm going to make it?"

"I just do," Becky said. "Trust me. I've been on the team for three years now. It's always obvious who's going to make it and who isn't."

"And your friends *aren't*," Lindsay added, nodding toward the table where Emily and Sarah were sitting.

"Sixth graders don't usually," Becky explained, "but you're special."

"And they are, too," Lindsay said with a smirk, still looking at Emily and Sarah. "Just in a *different* way." All of the girls around the table laughed, and Jenna joined in. She felt kind of bad about making fun of Emily and Sarah, but it wasn't like they would ever find out.

"Seriously," Marianne Moore jumped in.

She'd made the squad when she was in seventh grade. "I've never seen two more uncoordinated people. I mean"—she stretched her left arm above her head and her right arm across her chest while she made a goofy face—"what's *that* about? It's like they're totally clueless or something." Again, everyone at the table laughed, sneaking looks at Emily and Sarah as they did, and Jenna chortled along with them. She didn't think what Marianne said was funny, exactly, but she didn't want to stand out.

"What are you doing!" Max cried fluttering up from the yogurt container into Jenna's line of sight. "They're making fun of your friends! Aren't you going to stick up for them?"

*What? And lose my spot on the cheerleading team?* Jenna thought, looking straight through him. What did he expect from her? Max obviously knew nothing about middle-school politics. He hovered in front of her face for a minute, but Jenna continued to ignore him. Eventually, Max drifted back down to the yogurt, making a crinkling sound as he landed on its foil top.

Jenna was relieved her little winged buddy had stopped bugging her, but as the laughter died down, a question occurred to her. "Hey, Becky?" she started. "I know Sarah and Emily are like, way behind learning the cheers and stuff, but tryouts aren't until next week, right?"

"Yeah. So?"

"So, in a way, they still have a chance to make the team, right? I mean, if they pick up the cheers and really nail them in the next couple of days."

"I guess," Becky said, "but I don't think that's going to happen, do you? They're so far behind right now they might as well give up."

"Nice," Max said. "Is that the cheer they use when your team's behind? *Give it up, give it up, wayyyyyy up!*" he chanted, clapping his hands and jumping into the air.

Jenna pursed her lips and tried to ignore him. "But they *could* do really well at tryouts, right? And I could totally mess up. How can you be so sure that I'm going to make it? Aren't there like, five judges?"

Becky and Lindsay smiled knowingly at Jenna. "Yes, there are five judges," Becky said, "but you don't need to worry. Lindsay and I are on the panel, and we can really swing the vote."

"Really?" Jenna asked.

"Sure," Lindsay replied. "Coach Fine totally trusts us."

"Yeah, I could pretty much tell you who's going to make the team right now, and those two," Becky said, laughing as she pointed toward Sarah and Emily's table, "aren't on the list. They're horrible!"

Jenna was surprised. She knew that Becky and Lindsay would have a say in who got picked for the team, but she hadn't realized they would have so much power. Of course, having them in charge of the process did work in Jenna's favor.

She was pretty and popular—just the kind of cheerleader they would want—and Jenna had known from the beginning that her chances of making the team were good for those two reasons alone. Of course, it didn't hurt that she was talented, too, but she was fairly certain that if she'd had any trouble learning the cheers, one of the older girls would have stepped in to help her. But nobody was helping Emily and Sarah.

"Sarah and Emily are not horrible!" Max protested. His normally pink cheeks had turned bright red. "They just need some help," he added. Jenna knew he was right, but she wasn't about to say anything while everyone at the table was giggling.

In fact, the only thing Jenna felt that she could do was to laugh along with them. If she didn't, they might start to think she was just as immature and out of it as her friends were.

Besides, it wasn't like Emily and Sarah were right there or anything. And once Jenna made the team, she could make it up to them. But right now she had to focus on fitting in.

Becky and Lindsay held positions of power. They were the ones who were going to determine whether Jenna spent the next couple of months learning cheers and dance routines and performing in front of a crowded gymnasium or going straight home after school every day and watching the basketball games from the bleachers.

Jenna looked around the lunch table. These were the girls she needed to impress. They were the ones in charge of her future. What good would it do her—or anyone else—to get on their bad side?

# CHAPTER
## Eight

"You should have stood up for your friends!" Max argued as Jenna headed for the bathroom with him perched on her shoulder. Cheering practice was starting in ten minutes and Jenna needed to get her hair into two perfect pigtails. Jenna pushed open the door to the girls' bathroom, pleased to find it empty so that she could talk openly to Max.

"What difference would it have made if I had?" she said once they were inside. "It's not like Becky and Lindsay would have changed their minds about them."

"They may have," Max replied.

"As if," Jenna retorted. "They just would have decided that I was lame, too, and then *none* of us would have made the team."

"Team, shmeam!" Max said. "You simply must

begin treating your friends with a little respect if you want them to keep being your friends."

Jenna sighed. She was getting tired of her little winged friend, with all of his good advice and bad aim. "Well, maybe I *don't*," she said, pulling her brush through her long, dark hair and sectioning it off. "Once I make the team I'll probably be hanging out with the other cheerleaders most of the time, anyway. I probably won't even have time for Emily and Sarah."

"And *after* cheering season is over?" Max asked. "Just what do you suppose you'll do then?"

Jenna pressed her lips together. She hadn't really thought that far ahead. "I'll probably still hang around with Becky and Lindsay and the rest of the team," she answered. She wasn't exactly sure that was the way things would go, but Max didn't need to know that. "We'll probably all be good friends by then, and they're more my style anyway. You know—cool, popular, up on all the latest trends."

"You forgot shallow, superficial, and vain!" Max said.

Jenna gasped. "Is that what you think of me?" she asked.

"That's absolutely how I think you're acting right now."

"You're just upset because I haven't been

using my love rock to make the world a better place," Jenna sneered.

Max folded his arms and frowned. "It's not just me, Jenna. That's what your friends think of you these days, too," Max said.

Jenna shot him a sideways glance. "No they don't," she said. "I could go out there right now and ask them to hang out after practice and they'd say yes."

"Don't be so sure," Max said.

"What's that supposed to mean?"

"See for yourself, princess," Max told her. He fluttered down to the shelf above the sink where Jenna had set her ponytail holders. Then, as she was brushing through her hair, Max scooped up the two baby blue elastics and flitted toward the bathroom door.

"Hey! Give those back!" Jenna shouted. Max ignored her and flew straight at the door, managing to squeeze out through one of the vents. "You little—! What do you think you're doing? Come back here with those!" Jenna called, following him into the hallway, her brush still in her hand.

She jogged after the little cupid, but Max's wings were beating faster than she'd ever seen them go before and he was outdistancing her. Jenna wanted to call out to him, but there were still a few other students in the hallway, so she couldn't. She was just about to turn the corner into the sixth-grade wing when Max popped out from behind a fire extinguisher and stopped her. Jenna made a swipe for her hair bands, but Max snatched them away.

"Maximus Trebellius Whatevericus!" Jenna sneered in a whisper, "I'm going to—"

But Max shushed her before she could finish. "Quiet!" he hissed. "Just get over here and listen."

"To what?"

Max stared back at her, his large blue eyes looking fiercer than usual. "*Just. Follow. Me*," he commanded, and Jenna, not knowing what else to do, obeyed for once.

Cautiously, Max flew and Jenna crept to the other side of the hallway where they could hide behind a bank of lockers. Just a little ways down the hall, between Mrs. MacKnight's and Ms. Garcia's rooms, Keisha, Emily, and Sarah were having a conversation.

"We're really sorry, Keisha," Sarah was saying.

"We were totally wrong," Emily added. "It's just that, well, you know, she's *Jenna Scott*, one of the most popular girls in school. I guess we were kind of, I don't know—"

"—flattered that she wanted to spend time with us," Sarah finished.

"Yeah," Emily agreed. "That's true. We were. Plus she just seemed so nice and so cool and so fun. And I guess in a way we thought that hanging out with Jenna would make us popular, too."

"And it kind of did, for a while, but then we realized that it didn't matter," Sarah said. "What we really want is a good friend, and Jenna isn't one."

Jenna gasped. "Yes I am," she whispered. "Why would they say that?"

"Maybe because lately you've been more concerned with whether or not your pigtails are even than how your friends are doing."

"B-but," Jenna stammered, "I let them hang out with me for the last four months. I helped them pick out new clothes and restyle their hair. I had them over to my house after school and hung out with them at the mall and introduced them to the cool boys. How can they say I'm not a good friend? What else do they want from me?"

"Perhaps you should listen and find out." Max suggested. Jenna started to protest, but Max brought his index finger to his lips, silencing her once again. Jenna scowled. She didn't really want to hear any more of what her friends had to say, but at the same time, she couldn't tear herself away.

"Jenna ditched us as soon as cheerleading tryouts started," Sarah went on. "Once she saw that she had a chance to hang around with Becky and Lindsay and that whole crew, she didn't want anything to do with us."

"We thought she was nice and that she really liked us," Emily said. "But she's totally two-faced and all she cares about is being popular."

"You're just realizing that?" Keisha asked.

"I guess so," Sarah said.

"Because she ditched you to hang out with someone more popular?"

"Yup," Emily agreed. "She just forgot we even existed."

"That's funny," Keisha said, folding her arms across her chest. "Because that's exactly what you guys did to me at the beginning of the year."

Both Emily and Sarah stared at the ground. "We know," Emily said. "And we're really sorry."

"Jenna wasn't a good friend to us, and we weren't good friends to you," Sarah said. "But we're hoping you'll give us another chance."

"We've been friends for such a long time," Emily said. "Since we were all *five years old*."

"And we want to be friends again," Sarah said. "What do you think?"

Jenna peeked around the locker, watching as Keisha bit her lip, considering all of the things that Emily and Sarah had said to her. But before Keisha opened her mouth to speak, Max nodded to Jenna. "That's enough," he said. "Let's go."

Jenna took one last look down the hall and then followed the little cupid back to the bathroom. Once they were inside, Max placed her ponytail holders back on the shelf and Jenna automatically went to the mirror and began brushing her hair slowly, aware of a prickling sensation in her eyes.

*How could Emily and Sarah say those things about me? Have I really been that horrible to them?* Jenna looked up to see Max standing on the soap dispenser, his arms crossed and his face serious.

"Well? What do you think?" he asked.

Jenna wasn't sure what to think. She took a deep breath and discovered that her heart was beating rapidly. Emily and Sarah had said some really mean things about her—things that had hurt her. And she wasn't used to being hurt.

Glancing back in the mirror, Jenna began to brush her hair harder, with more purposeful strokes. Here she had been claiming that Emily and Sarah were such good friends that they would forgive her for just about anything. She felt so foolish.

"I think I should go back out there and let them know that I heard every word they said," Jenna snapped. "Where do they get off, talking about me like that anyway?"

"Jenna—"

"No, really. I mean, who do they think they are? They're calling *me* two-faced? What about them? They're the ones who—"

"Jenna!" Max yelled at the top of his lungs, and for such a tiny person he could make a lot of noise.

"What?" Jenna snapped.

"Calm down!" Max said in a quieter tone. "You need to—"

"Don't you dare tell me to get out that ridiculous rock!"

Max paused for a moment, sat down on the edge of the dispenser, and crossed his hands in his lap. "All right," he said quietly. "I won't. Although you could do with a tad bit more patience at the moment."

"Patient? You want me to be patient? Did you hear what they said?"

"I did," Max said, "and I think you should take a minute to think about it."

"No, I think I should just forget about it, and

forget about them, too. Cheerleading starts in three minutes and if I want to make the team I need to—"

"I, I, *I*, I, I," Max droned. "Can't you take just one minute to think about someone other than yourself? Think about what Emily and Sarah said. They were good friends to you. They enjoyed spending time with you, and they've been hurt by the way you treated them."

"The way *I* treated *them*? The only reason they hung out with me in the first place was so that they could be more popular. They used me."

"That's not true," Max said.

"Yes it is. That's what they just said."

"That's only part of what they said," Max corrected her. "They also said that they thought you were cool and nice and fun and that they thought you really liked them."

"I did!"

"But then you abandoned them."

"They abandoned *me*," Jenna argued.

"Only because of the way you treated them, Jenna," Max told her. "You've been ignoring them, avoiding them—you've even been making fun of them. How long did you expect them to stick around and put up with all of that?"

Jenna opened her mouth to deny Max's

accusations, but she was at a loss for words. She had ignored them, and avoided them, and yes, even made fun of them. But hadn't they just done the exact same things to her? More or less?

"Look," Jenna said, hardening her face in the mirror and rapidly brushing her hair into a second pigtail. "I'm not the bad guy here. Emily and Sarah haven't talked to me since break today—"

"When you told them that if they couldn't learn the cheers on their own they probably didn't belong on the team anyway."

Jenna squinted. Had she really said that? It did sound kind of familiar. "The point is," she said, "they've been rude to me, too."

"*Today*!" Max yelled. "They've been rude to you *today*! After putting up with you for who knows how long?"

"Why are you defending them?" Jenna asked.

"I'm not defending them," Max explained. "I'm just trying to get you to be honest with yourself."

Jenna finished brushing out her second pigtail and slammed the brush down on the stainless steel counter. She'd been gripping it so hard her knuckles had turned white, and her fingers felt cramped. But instead of taking a minute to calm herself down, Jenna plowed ahead, yanking the remaining half of her hair into position.

"You want me to be honest?" she asked, securing her second pigtail with a light-blue elastic and checking her face in the mirror one last time. "Fine. You want honest? Here's honest: I don't need Emily and Sarah."

Max dropped his head into his hands and moaned, but Jenna was undaunted. "The more I think about it," she went on, "the more I realize that they're just way too immature for me. They want my attention twenty-four seven, and I don't have that kind of time."

"Jenna, you're completely missing the point."

"Actually, I think I understand the point perfectly," Jenna said. "I need friends that will pull me up, not drag me down. Friends like Becky and Lindsay." She turned to the little cupid and gave him a tight-lipped smile. "So from now on, I'm not going to waste my time on people like Emily and Sarah. I have other friends to hang out with—cooler friends who understand me better, and I have you to thank for helping me realize that. Thank you, Max," Jenna said.

And with that she wheeled around and marched out of the girls' bathroom.

# CHAPTER
## Nine

The next day at lunch, Jenna forced herself to walk past her old table without so much as a glance. It was difficult not to look at her former friends, but Jenna was still angry with them. Plus, she was determined to ignore them the way that they'd been ignoring her.

Neither Emily nor Sarah had spoken to her all morning—not in homeroom, not in math, not in language arts or social studies. Jenna wasn't expecting them to try to talk to her at lunch, either, but it didn't matter. She wasn't planning on talking to them, either. She had plenty of other people to hang out with, including the two most popular girls in the school, Becky and Lindsay, whose table she was headed for now.

"Oh, hey, Jenna," Becky said when Jenna approached. It wasn't exactly the same warm greeting she'd gotten yesterday—Becky had barely looked up—but it would do.

"Can I sit here?" Jenna asked, nodding toward the stool across from Becky's.

"I think Liz is sitting there," Becky said.

"And Beth's sitting there," Lindsay said, pointing to the next stool. "I'm trying to set her up with Theo's best friend at Anderson, so we need to chat."

"Oh," Jenna said, sliding her tray down another seat.

"Actually, can you go one more?" Becky asked. "Danielle will want to sit next to Beth. They're like, best buds."

"Sure," Jenna replied, sliding down even farther. She felt kind of awkward sitting so far away from the two people she knew best at the table, but most of the other girls who'd be sitting there were on the cheerleading squad, too, so she was sure she'd get along well with them.

Once Jenna had taken her seat, Max hopped off her shoulder and perched himself on the edge of her tray. "So, did you see who was sitting with Sarah and Emily?" he asked. "*Keisha.*"

Jenna raised her eyebrows slightly, pretending to be surprised. Even though she'd kept herself from looking at them as she walked by, the truth was that she'd noticed Emily, Sarah, and Keisha—and Amanda and Sam, and Noah, Justin, and Luke—as soon as she'd stepped into the cafeteria. But Max didn't need to know that.

"Yep," he went on. "Keisha, Emily, and Sarah. It looks like they're friends again, after all. Pretty nice of Keisha to forgive them after they were so mean to her, but I suppose that's what friends do, hmm? Forgive one another?"

Jenna squinted down at the little cupid and frowned. She knew what he was trying to do and it wasn't going to work. She wasn't going to apologize to Sarah and Emily—they were the ones who should be apologizing to her. Not that she'd forgive them anytime soon. Jenna had moved on and she didn't have room for them in her life anymore. She had other friends now—a whole table full of them. Jenna looked around at the girls who had filled in the rest of the seats around her. She didn't know many of them very well, but in time, she was sure they'd all be great friends.

"Hey, Jenna," Becky called from three seats down. The chatter around the rest of the table stopped. When either Becky or Lindsay had something to say, everyone listened. "Did you see Sarah and Emily at practice yesterday? They were hysterical!"

"Talk about awkward," Lindsay said, making a goofy face.

"Yeah," Jenna said, managing a small chuckle to go along with the laughter of the rest of the table. She could feel Max staring at her with disapproval, so she avoided meeting his eyes.

"Don't these wonderful new friends of yours ever talk about anything else?" he asked.

*Of course they do,* Jenna thought, and she was going to prove it. "Hey—has anyone seen that new Joelle movie?" she asked, referring to her favorite teenage actress. "It looks really good."

Becky snorted. "You're kidding, right?" she asked.

"Um . . ." Jenna hesitated. Glancing around the table, she sensed that she had said something wrong. Everyone seemed to be wearing amused smiles, and none of them looked particularly friendly.

"You know who really likes Joelle?" Lindsay chimed in with the most amused smile of all. "My five-year-old niece! You can take her to see it if you want, Jenna," she offered and all of the girls laughed.

"Oh, no," Jenna stammered, feigning a smile. "I was only kidding. I can't stand Joelle. She's so . . . babyish."

"Totally," Danielle agreed. "I mean, I may have liked her when I was in like, fourth grade, but not now. Her movies are definitely aimed at little kids—there's never even any kissing."

"Yeah, totally," Jenna agreed, hoping she'd covered her blunder well enough.

Thankfully, most of the girls seemed to be letting it go, but Lindsay was eyeing her suspiciously. "So who *do* you like?" she asked, the amused smile still playing on her lips. "Who's your favorite actress, Jenna?"

There was silence at the table as everyone waited for Jenna's answer. Jenna racked her brain trying to come up with someone Becky, Lindsay, and the rest of them would approve of. She felt like she was being tested, like her answer to this question alone would determine whether or not she was welcomed back to the lunch table tomorrow afternoon.

Jenna's neck began to itch. As she reached up to scratch it, she remembered the name of an actress her brother's girlfriend had been raving about not too long ago. "Um, Scarlett Davidson?" she ventured.

"Oh, yeah, she's great," Becky said. "I really like her, too. Did anyone see her in—"

Jenna heaved a sigh of relief as the other girls continued to talk about the high points of

Scarlett Davidson's acting career thus far. In truth, Jenna wasn't really that fond of her, but she was glad she'd come up with an acceptable name, even if Lindsay had seemed disappointed when she did.

It seemed obvious that Lindsay wasn't as keen on having her hang out as Becky was, which meant that she was going to have to keep her guard up. If Lindsay had a chance to make her look like a fool, Jenna thought she might take it.

Able to relax for a moment, Jenna stabbed at the peas and corn on her tray.

"Oh, listen!" Max said, jumping up and down and clapping his hands like a little kid on Christmas morning. "Lindsay's talking about Theo again! Isn't that exciting? I just can't get enough of hearing about that guy!"

Jenna scowled at the little cupid. She was getting tired of his sarcasm, but even she had to admit that Theo wasn't the most compelling subject in the world. In fact, if it came down to a choice between being put on the spot again or listening to Lindsay gab on and on about Theo, Jenna would probably choose the former. And that's when it hit her.

Jenna glanced down at the little cupid in amazement. What was it he had said?

Something about Sarah and Emily acting their age while Jenna was pretending to be something that she wasn't. *And that's exactly what I'm doing,* Jenna realized.

Was this what it was going to be like hanging out with Becky and her friends all the time? Was Jenna always going to be stuck somewhere between boredom and anxiety?

Jenna glanced over at her old lunch table and sighed. Emily, Sarah, and Keisha were all laughing. Even Amanda and Sam seemed to be getting along with everyone just fine. And Noah, Justin, and Luke appeared to be up to their usual tricks—using their forks as catapults to launch green beans, corn, peas, and carrots at one another.

Who ever would have thought that Amanda Littlefield would be hanging out with some of the most popular kids in the sixth grade? Or that Sam Sullivan, that geeky seventh-grade outcast, would be joking around with someone as trendy and well-liked as Noah Carpenter? Most of all, who ever would have thought that Jenna Scott would want to trade places with either of them?

Jenna pushed her vegetables around on her plate and sighed. How had she let things get so messed up?

"It's not too late, you know," Max said. He'd obviously seen her staring longingly at her old gang and their new friends. "Sorry goes a long way toward making things better," he added, but Jenna wasn't so sure.

After the way she'd been ignoring Emily and Sarah—and all of the things she'd said to them lately—how could they ever forgive her? And she'd been mean to Amanda, Sam, and Keisha all year. How was she supposed to apologize for that? And Noah thought she was a total loser, which meant that his buddies probably did, too.

Jenna gazed down at Max and sighed. He was right that she owed Sarah and Emily an apology—she knew that now. But he was wrong about the other part. Sometimes it *was* too late.

# CHAPTER
## Ten

"Nice, Jenna!" Coach Fine called out from the center of the gym. "Now do it again." Jenna smiled at the compliment, but knew that she needed to keep working if she wanted to impress the cheerleading coach.

For the past week, Coach Fine had been in and out during practices—mostly out—letting Becky, Lindsay, and the other eighth-grade squad members run things. Becky said that it was because she trusted them so much that she was basically going to let them pick the team, but it seemed odd to Jenna to have a coach that was so hands-off.

Her theory was that Coach Fine was pregnant and experiencing terrible nausea. She'd seen her face turn practically white a few times before she'd rushed out of the gym, and it reminded Jenna of the way her aunt had looked when she was first pregnant with Jenna's cousin, Sierra.

She'd tried to share her theory with Becky and the others, but it was nearly impossible to get a word in edgewise with those girls. And most of the time when Jenna did manage to add something to the conversation, she ended up being dismissed.

Meanwhile, she'd watched from afar as Sarah, Emily, and Keisha had renewed their friendship, incorporating Amanda, Sam, Noah, Justin, and Luke into the mix. Jenna envied them so much, sitting across the cafeteria laughing and acting silly while she was trying desperately to act mature enough to fit in with her new eighth-grade friends.

Becky, Lindsay, and the others had more or less accepted Jenna into their fold in that they let her sit with them at lunch and hang out with them during break and at cheerleading practice, but she felt more like a little sister to them than a peer. In fact, over the weekend, Danielle had had a slumber party to which Jenna wasn't invited. She'd told Jenna that it was because her mom had made her limit it to eight friends and the invitations had all gone out before Jenna had started hanging out with them, but Jenna wasn't completely sure that was the whole story.

She knew that Becky liked her and that as long as that was true the others would put up with her whether they did or not. But Jenna was beginning to wonder if even Becky really thought that she was cool, or if she just thought Jenna was cool . . . *for a sixth grader.*

Max kept trying to persuade her to apologize to Sarah and Emily and get her real friends back, but Jenna couldn't bring herself to do it. They seemed perfectly happy without her in their lives, and as time passed, it seemed more and more unlikely that they would ever want to be her friends again.

So instead, Jenna had resigned herself to sitting through lunches dedicated to talking about Theo, guessing at who would make the cheerleading team, and making fun of everyone in the school who wasn't cool enough to be part of their clique. And in her free time, Jenna had put all of her energy into cheering.

"We're on the move, and out to prove / we're gonna win this game!" Jenna chanted as she practiced the movements that went with the cheer again. As usual, she hit everything perfectly and landed the jump at the end without a hop or even a wobble.

"Impressive!" Max called out from the bleachers. "Now go apologize to your friends."

Jenna just shook her head and got ready to do the cheer again. Everyone was practicing on their own for the moment, getting ready to do both cheers together one last time before tryouts.

"Okay!" Coach Fine yelled out, her deep voice filling the gym. If she had, in fact, been nauseated as Jenna suspected, she was obviously feeling much better today. "Everybody stop what you're doing for a moment and look at Jenna."

Jenna froze, worried that she'd done something wrong and was being used as an example of how *not* to cheer.

"Can you do that jump again, Jenna? The one at the end of Grapevine?"

"Sure," Jenna said. She took a step, circling her arms forward and then sprung upward to execute a flawless toe touch. Her legs were perfectly straight, stretched in a wide straddle, and her hands, which were in tight fists, reached just below her heels. And with the muscular legs she'd developed through dance and gymnastics, Jenna was able to clear four and a half feet easily.

"*That's* how it should look, people!" Coach Fine called. "Did you see that? Legs parallel to the floor, arms down, chin up? Remember that."

Jenna glanced toward the bleachers and

caught Max's eye. "Well, it certainly looks like you're going to make the team!" he called. "But you'll have to take the first step if you want your other little wish to come true." Jenna shook her head in disbelief. He was like a broken record.

She looked over at Emily and Sarah, who were on the other side of the gym practicing together. Their cheers looked better today, but there were still a few things they could tweak to make them better.

"Do you have your rose quartz?" Max called. Jenna reached into her pocket and felt the smooth surface of the pink love stone. *Patience and kindness,* she thought as she rubbed it. She certainly hadn't shown her friends much of either over the last month. If she had, maybe she'd be over there practicing with them. *But if I was practicing with them, I probably wouldn't make the team,* Jenna thought. Then again, if making the team meant spending all of her time with people she didn't enjoy, maybe it wasn't worth it.

Jenna shook her head again and tried to push all of the confusing thoughts from her mind. She didn't have time to try to figure it all out now. She needed to practice.

"Why do they keep coming back?" Jenna heard Danielle say to Beth. She stuffed the stone back in her pocket and went back to cheering, listening in on the two eighth graders as she did.

"I don't know. It's pathetic," Beth replied. "Nice jump, Sarah!" she called across the gym, and then she and Danielle nearly collapsed laughing.

Jenna glanced sideways at them. There were two people who could stand to learn a little patience and kindness. And she could think of at least six more—all of the eighth graders she'd been hanging around with lately could use a few remedial manners lessons.

"Did you hear that, Jenna?" Beth asked, still giggling.

"Yeah, I heard it," Jenna said, starting Grapevine over again.

"I swear, I think they get worse every day," Danielle said with a giggle.

Jenna pressed her eyes closed and tried to focus on the cheer. Why did they have to keep picking on Sarah and Emily anyway?

"You know why they do it, don't you?" Max called out from the bleachers. Jenna stopped dead and stared at the little cupid. It was as if he'd read her mind. "It makes them feel better about themselves," Max went on. "They put other people down in order to raise themselves up."

Jenna turned around and glanced at Danielle and Beth, who were still giggling and making fun of the sixth graders. Then she looked over at Sarah and Emily, who were doing their best to master the cheers without any help.

"Is that what you want to be, Jenna?" Max shouted to her. "A person who has to make fun of other people in order to feel good about herself?"

Jenna gazed at Lindsay and Becky, the two perfect eighth graders, and thought about all of the perfectly boring lunchtimes she'd had with them over the last week. Then she looked over at Sarah and Emily, the two imperfect sixth graders who'd giggled with her and hung out with her and not cared if she liked Joelle or cartoons or TV shows made for little kids. Next, she looked back at Danielle and Beth, mocking Sarah and Emily because it was better to *have* a target than to *be* a target.

*No,* she thought. *That's not what I want to be.* And then she walked straight across the gym to where Sarah and Emily were standing, still practicing even though they knew the older girls were laughing at them.

"Jenna," Emily said. "What are you doing over here? Don't you know? This is the unpopular side of the gym."

"Yeah, you better go back with your friends before they start to think you're a loser, too," Sarah added.

"Look, I don't expect you to believe me, but I'm sorry for the way I treated you. I was wrong and I know it," Jenna said. "But that's not why I came over here."

Sarah and Emily squinted at her. "Then why did you?" Sarah asked.

"To help you."

Emily laughed. "We don't want your help and we don't need it, Jenna," she sneered.

"Yes, you do," Jenna replied, "and whether you want it or not, you're getting it." Emily started to protest, but Jenna cut her off. "The first thing you both need to do is square your feet and turn your palms in. Sarah, you're pigeon-toed, and Emily, you're crow-toed. Either way, it looks horrible whenever you step your legs apart. You need to make sure your toes are pointing forward, like this, and if you have to take smaller steps to make that happen, that's okay. Just get your feet straight."

Jenna knelt down and moved both Emily's and Sarah's feet into the proper positions and then stood up and surveyed them. "That's it," she said. "Right there. Practice keeping your feet just like that."

Sarah and Emily were both staring at Jenna with bewildered expressions, but Jenna didn't let that stop her. They needed a lot of help and she was short on time. "As for your hands, keep your fingers pressed together tight and turn your palms in toward your body at all times unless you need to do something special with them during a cheer."

She adjusted their hands, and then pulled both of their arms straight out in front of them. "And this," she said, tapping the insides of their elbows. "*No bends.* Your arms need to be tight. They can't be flailing around like spaghetti. Think straight, crisp—like poles. They only bend when you make them bend."

As Jenna continued, Sarah and Emily began to listen more intently, leaning forward and nodding at everything she said. "Hey, you two!" Jenna called to Michelle Burton and Lucy Greene, who were practicing a few feet away. "You might as well get over here, too."

Lucy and Michelle walked over slowly, confused at first as to why Jenna wanted them, but when she started handing out more advice they stood up straight and took note.

"Keep your head level," Jenna told them all. "Don't let it bob around all over the place—that looks sloppy. And when you do a jump, only go as high as you can go with good form. And always stick the landing. Nothing looks worse than—"

"Jenna?" Becky interrupted.

Jenna turned to see that both Lindsay and Becky were behind her. "Yes?"

"What are you doing?" Lindsay asked.

"I'm helping these girls," Jenna replied. Then she turned back to Sarah, Emily, Michelle, and Lucy and continued her talk. "Nothing looks worse than falling out of your landing and stumbling—"

"*Jen-na*," Becky said again. "Everyone is supposed to be practicing on their own right now."

Jenna turned around again and sighed. "I know," she said, "but Danielle and Beth pointed out to me that these sixth graders were a little behind so I thought I'd help them."

"That's not your job," Lindsay said, narrowing her eyes at Jenna.

"Well, I didn't see anyone else doing it," Jenna said, narrowing hers right back. "Besides," she said, turning her gaze to Becky, "I want to be a good cheerleader, and I thought that's what cheerleaders did—help to spread school spirit. And what better way to spread school spirit than to help out my fellow students?"

"You're not a cheerleader yet," Lindsay sneered.

"No, and neither are my friends here," Jenna replied. "But we'd all like to give it a shot, so if you'll excuse us, we have some more practicing to do." Jenna turned back to the sixth graders, but she could feel Lindsay fuming behind her.

"You are such a—"

"Come on, Lindsay," Becky said, tugging on her friend's elbow. "Let's go see how the seventh graders are doing."

Jenna waited for a minute, listening for their footsteps, and when she heard them walking away, she took a deep breath and focused on the four girls in front of her. "Okay, voice," she said. "It's important that you work on making your voice loud without letting it get too high. If you do that, you'll—"

"Jenna?" Emily interrupted.

"What?"

"Thanks."

"Yeah, thanks," the other three girls echoed.

Jenna shook her head and stared down at her feet. "I should have done it a long time ago," she said.

"Better late than never," Sarah said.

Jenna glanced up to see that Sarah was smiling at her and she felt tears beginning to well up in her eyes. "I guess," she said, blinking rapidly. "But I still wish I'd done it last week. I've been such a snob, you guys. I wouldn't blame you if you never forgave me."

"We can talk about forgiveness later," Emily said. "But right now we have some cheers to learn."

"Right," Jenna said, grinning back at her friends. She glanced over her shoulder at Max, who was happily fluttering though loop de loops in the air over the bleachers.

"Love stone!" he yelled out, cupping his hands to his mouth. Jenna reached in the pocket of her shorts and felt the smooth pink rock she'd been carrying everywhere for the last five days. She rubbed it between her thumb and forefinger, feeling its smooth surface and the gentle curve of its sides. And for the first time, she thought she understood what Max had been trying to tell her. Love, patience, and kindness. Maybe it wasn't such baloney after all.

# CHAPTER
## Eleven

During her tryout the next afternoon, Jenna nailed both of her cheers. They were absolutely flawless, she knew, but she also knew that that didn't necessarily mean she had made the squad. Lindsay hadn't looked impressed at all when she finished, and Jenna wasn't sure where Becky stood.

As she exited the music room, Jenna felt more nervous than she had before tryouts had begun, because now all she could do was wait. Thankfully, she was one of the last people to go, so the list announcing who had made the squad should be going up fairly soon.

"How'd you do?" Sarah asked as Jenna walked over to join her and Emily by the water fountain.

"Pretty well, I think," Jenna said. "How about you guys?"

"Way better than I would have without all of your tips," Emily said.

"Yeah, me, too," Sarah agreed, "but I still don't think I made it."

"Don't say that, Sarah," Jenna told her. "You never know."

Sarah shrugged. "Actually, I'm pretty sure," she said. "But it's okay. I mean, I didn't really expect to make it this year anyway. I just wanted to try out so I'd know what it was like. That way if I decide to try out again next year I'll be more prepared."

"That's kind of how I feel, too," Emily said.

"You guys," Jenna moaned. "You're supposed to be optimistic."

"We're just being realistic, Jenna," Emily said. "I'd love it if I made the team, but I'm not counting on it. You should make it, though," she added. "You're definitely one of the best cheerleaders around."

"And the nicest," Sarah added.

"Yeah, well that's not saying much," Jenna replied, thinking about how rude some of the eighth graders had been to Sarah and Emily.

"They're not all bad," Emily said.

"No, I guess not," Jenna said. After all, Andrea and Molly would probably make the team and they were pretty nice, and there were bound to be others. And as Jenna knew, sometimes even the snobbiest ones could change for the better.

She glanced back at the music room door where tryouts were being held and tapped her foot. "I feel like this is taking forever," she said. "I think I'm going to go wait in the gym. Do you want to come?"

"No, Michelle and Lucy are the last two people trying out. I think I'm going to wait here for them," Emily said.

"Me, too," Sarah added.

"Okay, but will you guys come get me when the list goes up?" Jenna asked.

"Sure," Emily replied. "And Jenna? Thanks again."

"No problem," Jenna said. "I owed you one. At *least*."

As she trotted down to the gym, Jenna felt lighter than she had in a long time. She was really hoping she would make the cheerleading team, but whether she did or not, it was nice to know she had good friends who would stand by her. Even better was knowing that she was strong enough to stand by them now, too.

"Hey, did you forget something back there in the music room?" a small voice called as Jenna reached the gym.

"Ohmigosh—Max!" she gasped, turning around. The tiny cupid was soaring down the hallway behind her, his little wings flapping for all they were worth. When he caught up to her, he alighted on her shoulder and gave her a stony stare.

"I'm *so* sorry, Max," Jenna gushed. "I totally forgot to grab you on my way out."

"Quite alright!" Max replied. "I understand. You were excited—and you should be. You were great in there. I think you might have made the team!"

"Really?"

"Sure," the cupid said with a wave of his small hand. "I'd pick you. You were—ooh! Noah, twenty feet away and closing!" he shouted suddenly, grabbing the green arrow from his quiver and stringing it on his bow.

"What?" Jenna asked, peering into the gym. She saw Noah Carpenter heading straight toward her. Actually, he was headed for the water fountain just inside the gym door, and Max was already getting ready to shoot him! He pulled the arrow back, lined up his shot, and—

"Wait!" Jenna breathed. "Don't!" She reached up and grabbed the arrow away from Max, nearly knocking him over.

"What are you doing?" Max asked. "That was the clearest shot I've had of him all week!"

"I know," Jenna said. "I guess I've just . . . changed my mind."

"What on earth do you mean? Don't you like him anymore?" Max asked.

"Sure I do," Jenna replied, "but he doesn't like me."

"He would if you'd let me shoot him!"

"Yeah, but . . . I don't know," Jenna said. "It just doesn't seem like the right thing to do. I mean, Keisha likes him and he likes her, not me. And yes, I know the arrow would change that, but only for a little while, and then he'd probably go back to liking Keisha again."

"Maybe," Max said. "But you never know."

Jenna shrugged. "I guess I just feel like if he's ever going to like me, I want it to be real, you know? Not because he's under some kind of spell or something. What's the point of having someone fall in love with you if he doesn't really mean it?"

All at once, Max threw himself at Jenna's neck. "I'm so proud of you!" he cried, giving her the biggest hug he could with his tiny arms. Jenna giggled as the little cupid's wings tickled her neck. "This is tremendous! You've learned so much!"

She laughed as the little cupid planted a series of tiny pecks on her cheek. "Yeah, I guess I have," she said when he finished. "And I owe it all to you."

"Aw, shucks," Max said, his rosy cheeks turning even pinker than usual.

"It's true," Jenna said. "But you know what? There's still one more thing I have to do."

"What's that?" the little cupid asked.

Jenna reached into the front pocket of her gray hooded sweatshirt and pulled out the silver charm bracelet that she'd found in the gym— the one that belonged to Amanda and Keisha. "I have to return this," she said, nodding toward Keisha, who was sitting on the bleachers doing her homework while she watched Noah's practice.

"You know, Jenna," Max said, "there's one more thing I have to do, too."

"What?" Jenna asked.

"You see that bell up there?" he said, pointing to the ceiling of the gym. Way up above one of the climbing ropes at the other end of the gym was a tiny silver bell that people could ring if they climbed all the way to the top.

"Yeah," Jenna said.

"Well, watch this!" Max said. He took an arrow out of his quiver, expertly strung it in his bow, and let it fly. A second or two later, Jenna heard a *clang* and saw the little bell swinging. Her mouth dropped open.

"Did you do that?" she asked.

Max nodded proudly.

"But . . . how? You're a lousy shot."

Max tilted his head to the side and gave Jenna a crooked smile. "Sometimes yes, and sometimes no," he said.

"I don't believe you!" Jenna exclaimed. "You could have shot Noah at any time, couldn't you? You were missing on purpose!"

The little cherub threw back his head and laughed, and Jenna chuckled, too. She'd been so frustrated by Max's poor marksmanship, but it turned out it was all an act. "Oh, well," she said, "I guess I deserved that. And Keisha deserves this," she said, jingling the bracelet in her pocket.

"Hey, Keisha!" she called as she walked over to the bleachers.

Keisha pressed her lips together and sort of winced. "Jenna," she said. "What's up?" Jenna tried not to take her lack of enthusiasm personally. She knew she still had a lot to make up to Keisha—and Amanda and Sam—but hopefully returning the bracelet would be a step in the right direction.

"I think I found something of yours," Jenna said, pulling the bracelet from her sweatshirt pocket.

"The charm bracelet!" Keisha exclaimed, taking the bracelet from Jenna's hands. "Ohmigosh! Where did you find it?"

"On the gym floor," Jenna said.

"Wow! I can't believe it didn't get swept up or stepped on or anything," Keisha said. "It's been missing for over a week now. I can't wait to tell Amanda that you found it! She's going to be so psyched. Thanks, Jenna!"

"No problem," Jenna said. She glanced at her shoulder expecting to see Max there smiling back at her, but he was gone. *Maybe he snuck into one of my pockets,* Jenna thought, checking them all, but the only thing she could find was a tiny piece of paper.

She pulled it out of her pocket and unfolded it, realizing as she did that it was in the shape of a heart—a tiny heart—and there was a message on the front.

*Dear Jenna,*

*Congratulations on making the right choices—I knew you could do it! It's been fun hanging out with you, but I have to get back to work now. Good luck with cheerleading, and remember—carry your love stone*

*with you everywhere you go! It will help you*
*to remember what's important.*

*Love, patience, and kindness,*
*Marcus Trebellius Maximus*

As Jenna read the note, her heart sank. Max was gone and she hadn't even had a chance to say good-bye to him.

"Hey, Jenna!" Keisha called, bringing Jenna back to reality. "Did you add this?" she asked, holding up the bracelet.

Jenna squinted and took the bracelet back to examine it. All the charms that had been there when she'd first found it were still there, but now there was an extra one.

"Rose quartz," Jenna muttered, running her finger along the smooth stone.

"What did you say?" Keisha asked.

"It's rose quartz," Jenna repeated. "Or love stone—at least, that's what a friend of mine calls it."

"But where did it come from?" Keisha asked.

Jenna gazed up at her for a moment and the two of them exchanged secretive grins. "It came from me," Jenna replied. The corner of Keisha's mouth curved upward ever so slightly as she accepted the bracelet back, and suddenly Jenna was struck with the thought that not only was the bracelet magic, but that Keisha knew all about it.

She had about a thousand and one questions she wanted to ask Keisha, but before she got a chance, Emily and Sarah came bounding into the gym squealing.

"What is it?" Jenna asked. "Did you make the team?"

"No," Emily said, smiling nonetheless.

"But you did!" Sarah exclaimed. "Congratulations!"

Jenna felt a huge surge of excitement and energy wash over her. "Wow, thanks you guys!" Jenna said, hugging them both, "but I wish you'd made it, too."

Emily shrugged. "Yeah, but it's okay. You can teach us all the cheers and we'll try again next year."

"You've got a deal!" Jenna said, pleased to have her two best friends back again. *And,* she thought glancing over at Keisha, *I may even have found a new one.*